"You're a d

space cadet."

David's eyes sparkled with laughter. "A loose cannon in a chicken hat..."

"I am not."

"...and one hell of a nuisance," he added, ignoring Kelly's interruption.

She couldn't deny his last complaint. Not after he'd practically bailed her out of jail. "So go ahead. Laugh."

"Not today, Kelly." Gray eyes fixed on the road, he brushed her arm with the back of his knuckles, then concentrated on his driving.

With a grateful sigh, she accepted the temporary truce and closed her eyes. Then it hit her—he'd used her first name. A flush of warmth spread out from her center in slow ripples.

She opened her eyes when the truck stopped to let a car turn across traffic. "Where are we going?" she asked in sudden alarm.

"I'm taking you home."

Dear Reader,

I grew up in Texas, land of beefsteak and BBQ. And like David Whittaker, the hero of *Pure and Simple*, I think food's a sensual pleasure—that's all kinds of food. And I'd have to agree with Mr. Tuttle that if potato chips aren't a vegetable, well, they ought to be.

But most of the time, yes, I do try to eat green. Vegetarian cooking isn't simply the healthy choice. It's a pure and simple—and very sensual—pleasure.

The peanut sauce recipe that follows is one of my favorites. I've used it as a sauce on both hot and cold pasta and it makes a wonderful dressing for a cucumber and bean sprout salad.

PEANUT SAUCE

2 tsp soy sauce
2 tsp honey
2 tsp white or rice vinegar
2 tbsp peanut butter
2 tbsp sesame seed paste (tahini) or substitute more peanut butter
¾ tsp Chinese hot oil or chili oil (or crushed red-pepper flakes to taste)
2 cloves garlic, minced
½ tsp fresh ginger, minced
4 tbsp (approximately) brewed tea

Combine all ingredients and stir. Adjust seasonings to taste. Add enough brewed tea to thin the sauce to a creamy, pourable consistency. Enjoy!

Sincerely,

Peggy Nicholson

PURE AND SIMPLE

Peggy Nicholson

Harlequin Books

TORONTO • NEW YORK • LONDON
AMSTERDAM • PARIS • SYDNEY • HAMBURG
STOCKHOLM • ATHENS • TOKYO • MILAN
MADRID • WARSAW • BUDAPEST • AUCKLAND

To Jan, sister-in-law extraordinaire
With much gratitude to Nancy Cary, School Lunch Director of the Swansea, Massachusetts Public Schools, for showing me how a lunch program should be run (so that I might imagine how one should not). And to Dorothy Reney, Head Cook of Case Junior High School, and her wonderful "lunch ladies," Lorraine, Alice, Betty and Claudette—thank you for welcoming me into your kitchen. And Antoinette, thanks again, thanks always.

ISBN 0-373-03250-1

Harlequin Romance first edition February 1993

PURE AND SIMPLE

Printed in U.S.A.

CHAPTER ONE

SOME WOMEN WEAR HATS to be fashionable. Others wear hats to shield their heads from rain or sun. Kelly Bouchard wore hats as a disguise. For protective coloration. To proclaim her mood, or in hopes of changing it. Tonight, as she followed her fellow townspeople up the front steps of West Dartmouth High School, she was wearing her courage hat.

She glanced anxiously over her shoulder at the crowd closing in behind. *So many people.* She'd gotten up the nerve for the coming ordeal by telling herself that few citizens would attend this session of the school committee. For on a cold, blustery March night, how many people would want to leave their cozy living rooms to take part in a discussion of next year's school budget?

Apparently in West Dartmouth, at least half the town.

"You gonna just stand there, lady?"

Kelly blinked and found herself looking down on the bald head of a middle-aged man. "Oh!" She wheeled to find that the crowd had thinned ahead and that she was indeed blocking the inner doorway. "Oh—sorry!" She skittered ahead of him, stepped to the side and stopped again. Her slender freckled hands crept to the brim of her hat in a gesture of despair. If half the town was waiting outside to get in, the other half was already inside, milling noisily around the lobby. Kelly lifted her hat off her flaming, frizzy curls, then settled it again at a steeper angle with its brim almost brushing her small, freckled nose. She couldn't do it. She hadn't stood up in front of an audience since her high-school-drama days.

And things had been different, back in those painful times. That hadn't really been her—hadn't been big, shy, overweight Mount Kelly, as the other kids had called her, standing up on stage and speaking. It had been a character—Helen Keller's mother or the mayor's bossy wife in *The Music Man*.

But it would be different tonight if she stood up to speak. She would have no role to hide behind, beyond that of concerned parent and newly registered voter in the town of West Dartmouth. She couldn't do it. Sweeping off her hat again, she stared down at it absently while she crushed it between her fingers. It reminded her of the one Ingrid Bergman had worn to the airport at the end of *Casablanca*. A hat of courage and fierce resolve, to be worn by a woman turning her back on her lover, flying off instead to fight the good fight.... Kelly jammed the hat back on her head. Well, somebody had to fight this one.

As she'd dithered, much of the crowd had begun filing through the doors that led to the auditorium. By the entrance that Kelly approached, a gray-haired couple stood in conversation with a man wearing a corduroy jacket. The woman patted his arm. "We certainly will vote for the new school, Mr. Whittaker," she assured him. "Our oldest grandson is in junior high. These double sessions are terrible! Kids shouldn't have to walk home in the dark." Shaking her head, she followed her husband down the aisle.

Whittaker watched her go, a faint smile giving his lean face a look of inward satisfaction. As Kelly edged past him, he turned abruptly. "Hello." His voice was low and pleasant, his eyes a startling pale gray in his tanned face. "I haven't seen you here before."

"N-no. I mean, yes! You haven't." She and Suki had moved to West Dartmouth only the month before. There'd been no time, what with setting up the store, to be civic-minded. There was really no time now, but—

"David Whittaker." His hand came up to block her way. "I'm on the school committee."

That explained his friendliness. Every new face was a potential vote. She'd forgotten what small-town politics was like after so many years of living in Boston. "Kelly Hol—" She stopped, as she heard herself start to babble her married name. After six months she still forgot when she was rattled. "Bouchard," she amended as his fingers closed around hers.

His ice-gray irises had rims of navy blue, which gave his eyes a piercing look. Or perhaps it was his brows that made him look almost fierce when he wasn't smiling. Darker than his straight brown hair, they were two emphatic slashes rising toward his temples, rather than the usual gentle arcs. "Good to meet you, Kelly. I hope you came tonight to support the new high school we want to build?"

"Only if she wants our taxes raised." Leland Howard, Kelly's landlord and president of the West Dartmouth Town Council, stood at their side. He gave Whittaker a smile that revealed most of his glossy white teeth.

Whittaker didn't return it. "It'll raise the rates a dollar per thousand, Leland, if that. The town can handle it. And you know as well as I do that the school's desperately needed."

"I'm afraid I don't know that. Neither does Kelly, nor any other fiscally responsible voter in West Dartmouth." Leland slipped his hand through the crook of Kelly's elbow. "Come along, my dear, before all the seats are taken. David..."

Glancing back at the school-committee man, Kelly found her apologetic smile answered by a thoughtful frown. Then Whittaker swung away to buttonhole another arrival.

"I'm glad you decided to come tonight," Leland said at her ear. "Do you plan to speak up about that little matter we discussed?"

"Well, I..." If she said yes, there'd be no way to back out if her courage failed entirely.

"You really should, Kelly," her landlord urged for perhaps the tenth time this week. "Why, only this morning I was eating a bowl of yogurt and I got to thinking, Those poor kids... It's really a worthwhile cause...."

"Yes, it is," Kelly agreed, but why did she have to be the one to bring it up? With his place on the town council, surely Leland Howard was a better candidate to swing public opinion? That was why she'd first approached him, the day Suki got sick at school. And it was he who had suggested this forum for her complaint.

"Excuse me, my dear, that's the head of Zoning over there." He nodded at a man who was waving from the other side of the auditorium. "He seems to want me."

Kelly nodded and sank into an aisle seat. Nervous as she was, she was just as happy to sit by herself. Though Leland was all she could ask for in a landlord, somehow she'd not warmed to the man. "Smooth" was the word that came to mind when she thought of him. But then, wouldn't that apply to all politicians? Her eyes followed the figure of David Whittaker mounting the steps to join the other school-committee members on the dais, and she changed her mind. "Smooth" was not the word for Whittaker. "Hard" perhaps, but not "smooth." There'd almost been a touch of contempt in his eyes when she'd walked away from him—or had she imagined that?

Whittaker took the center seat at the long table, pulled a microphone into position and waited for silence. "Good evening," he said. "I'll be serving as acting chairman tonight. As was advertised in the *Dartmouth Daily,* this is an informational workshop. We'll start the actual preparation for the coming year's school budget next week. And of course you'll all be voting to accept or reject that budget in May, at the financial town meeting. But before we start crunching numbers, we wanted to get input from you people, the parents and taxpayers."

The crowd's rumble seemed to express equal parts approval and resentment. "I'll give you input!" the woman next to Kelly muttered.

"Before we ask for speakers, however, I want to say this." Whittaker's smile faded as his pale eyes scanned the room. "We all know what the real issue is here tonight. We need a new high school. We've needed it for four years now, and for four years a very small but very, umm, *vocal* faction of the voters has defeated the bond to finance it."

"And we'll keep on defeating it!" a man yelled from the rear of the room.

"Oh, shut up, Joe!" a woman's clear voice responded wearily.

Whittaker smacked a gavel on the table. The staccato clap made everyone jump. "You'll get your chance to vote however you please in May," he reminded them. "But tonight, I'd just like to say that these are *your* kids who are crammed thirty-five to a classroom in this building, a place that was built in the forties and hasn't been renovated since. These are *your* kids who have been on double sessions for four years, their school day shortened from the normal length by two hours.

"And this school district is due for its ten-year evaluation by the New England Association of Schools and Colleges next fall.

"It's going to fail its accreditation if we can't show them that we have a new school in the works, people. Without that accreditation, your kids haven't a prayer of being admitted to a decent college."

"Aw, you're breaking my heart!" growled Kelly's neighbor.

Kelly pulled that side of her hat down and shifted away from the woman. To her mind, Whittaker was talking sense. Children were the future, whether they were your own or someone else's. For the good of all they had to be properly educated. She was just glad that this wouldn't affect her own eight-year-old daughter. Surely by the time Suki was ready for junior high, the bond issue would have passed.

"The school-construction bond is, of course, separate from the regular school budget," Whittaker reminded them. "But here's what we hope you'll keep in mind tonight as we discuss possible cuts or additions to that budget. Money is tight—there's no doubt about that. So, since we're asking the town to vote yes on that bond issue, the school committee wants to do the best it can to hold down regular education costs wherever possible. We don't mean to spend one extra penny on frills or unessential items next year. We've persuaded the teachers' union to accept a one-year contract at *exactly* the same rate they're getting this year—a wage freeze, in other words. No raises, no move to the next step."

The crowd burst into enthusiastic applause.

"Hey, the bums are overpaid, anyway!" a rough voice yelled above the ovation, to be instantly answered by a spreading hiss of outrage.

Whittaker gaveled them all into silence. "That's how much a new high school and a renovated junior high means to your kids' teachers," he said calmly. "So tonight, we're asking you to match their concern. If you're proposing any expenditure that isn't essential, then *please,* don't even bring it up. This is a year for the basics, people, and nothing but. And now, if you still want to speak..."

Kelly let out a long, shaky breath while Whittaker accepted the first speaker and invited him to step down to the microphone placed below the stage. This was going to be even worse than she'd feared.

At the microphone, a short fat man was saying something about high-school-band uniforms...frayed at the collar...a disgrace to the town...baggy knees...the whatchamacallits—the epaulets—falling off... Why, in the homecoming game last October, he didn't have to remind anybody that the bandleader had taken a bow at halftime and split the seat of his trousers in front of the whole world.... The town of North Dartmouth wasn't going to let them forget *that* for the next twenty years! Remember the photo they ran in their paper? And on top of that, North Dartmouth had won the game—probably because of that! Why, the loss in morale...

Kelly pulled her courage hat even lower about her ears and closed her eyes. She wasn't seeing a disgraced bandleader in her mind's eye, but her mother, ten years ago, her normally ruddy, cheerful face white and as limp as a deflated balloon against the hospital pillow. A heart attack at age forty... "Only to be expected," the doctor had told Kelly, "as overweight as she is." His tired eyes passed over Kelly's blimplike figure and shied away. "We'll pull her through this one, but if she doesn't do something about it, she'll be back here within the year. She's *got* to slim down...."

Kelly opened her eyes and looked down at her slender hands. Absently she smoothed one hand up her arm and found its slim, muscled length reassuring. That was all behind her now. She was no longer Mount Kelly, at least in girth, and her mother—she smiled—her mother was down to a size eight and walked five miles every day.

But there had been no need for those years of humiliation Kelly had endured as a child. No need for her mother's brush with death. If she could save even one child from that—

"Thank you, Mr. Smith," Whittaker said firmly.

The band booster stopped in midsentence and turned to look up at Whittaker. He swung back to the voters. "But all I'm saying is—"

"Thank you. We'll certainly take it into consideration."

While Smith trudged back to his seat with an aggrieved shake of his head, two other townspeople started for the microphone. Whittaker pointed his gavel at the woman in the lead. "We'll take you first, Mrs. Leone, but if you'll wait one moment..."

The seven school-committee members conferred, leaning first to whisper to one neighbor, then the other. Heads were shaken, shrugs exchanged, solemn faces grew stern. Whittaker nodded, looked up and reached for his microphone. "Mr. Smith, we'll speak with the head of the music department about your concerns, but we can tell you this—there will be *no* increase in the music-department budget. There will probably be a substantial decrease. I understand that the piano used for choir practice by both junior and senior highs is on its last legs. If you or anyone else could help out by donating a usable upright, then possibly..."

It went on like that for almost an hour. Concerned parents alternated with speakers who complained bitterly about their property tax rates and demanded massive cuts in the budget. One frail-looking elderly woman proposed canceling the entire sports program—"Let 'em play sandlot baseball after school like the kids did when I was a girl!"—and was roundly booed by the audience.

Kelly alternately twisted her hat and rearranged it on her head. This wasn't a gentle or patient audience. They recognized no shades of gray. Everyone was passionately for or fanatically against. She couldn't imagine what they'd say to her proposal. She looked up with a start as Whittaker gaveled a speaker into silence.

"If the Science Club wants to go to the Smithsonian, Mr. Piper, they'll have to pay for their own transportation. School buses will be used only for basic services next year." He scanned the room. "Anyone else?"

It was time, if she was going to do it at all. Across the room, Leland Howard, sitting with his zoning friend, gave her a meaningful glance. He flicked his fingers in an encouraging little "get up there" gesture.

Her heart was smacking against her rib cage like a tennis ball being played off a backboard. She couldn't do it.

"Good," Whittaker was saying with obvious relief. "Then let's get on to the main order of business. We've prepared some charts on the costs of the new high school. I'm afraid the figures have gone up again since we presented them last year, but—"

"Wait!" Kelly croaked as she stood.

Whittaker looked up in annoyance. "We're past the proposal period, Ms. Boucher?"

"Bouchard," Kelly said in a half-strangled voice that didn't carry three rows. Her stomach whirled like a pitcher of stirred iced tea. She'd risen too quickly and her blood didn't seem to be making its usual lengthy ascent to her brain, which floated some five feet ten inches above the shabby auditorium carpet. The upturned, staring faces of the surrounding crowd seemed miles below her and alarmingly dim. Kelly pulled her hat down to shut them out. "I want to speak," she said, louder this time.

She'd felt this stage fright many times before, though not since her days as a high-school character actress. But the old reflexes kicked in. You took a deep breath, opened your mouth and the words would come tumbling from somewhere....

"Thank you," said Whittaker as she made it to the microphone, "but—"

She snatched at the device as much for support as to be heard, and nearly knocked it over. She saved it with a squeak of dismay, which the microphone caught and bounced off the back wall. Somebody snickered.

Whittaker's voice took on an edge. "I said the time for proposals is—"

"Oh, let her speak!" called a bored voice, which Kelly recognized as belonging to her landlord. "She's a voter, isn't she?"

"Right!" someone else called.

"Thank you," Kelly said automatically. She pulled off her hat and this time its back brim caught in her hair clip. The clip gave with a metallic *crack* that made her jump. Released from its tight French twist, her hair sprang out in a frizzy red halo around her head. Two or three people chuckled.

"Thank you," Kelly said again, as Whittaker made no further move to stop her. She passed her hat from one hand to the other, then without thinking, jammed it back on her head. Blithely unaware that she now resembled a Raggedy Ann who'd stuck her finger in an electrical socket, she addressed the audience. "Mr. Whittaker has asked us to keep to the basics tonight, but what I want to talk about is the most basic thing of all. I want to talk about...*food.*"

Someone laughed outright and Kelly tugged at her hat, pulling it down over her nose. She tilted up her chin so she could see her audience from beneath its comforting shelter. "I have an eight-year-old-daughter, Suki, and Suki usually takes her lunch to school. But the other day she traded it for a little friend's cafeteria lunch."

"Could we get to the point?" Whittaker said impatiently.

She flashed him an indignant glance that snagged on his cold gray gaze. With an effort she tore her eyes away just as a giggle rippled across the audience. "The point is that she threw it right up again."

"So she tossed her cookies, so what?" called Joe, the loudmouth on every issue.

Kelly flipped up the front brim of her hat to glare in his general direction. "So, when I realized that Suki wasn't ill, that it was the food itself that had made her sick, I started looking at the menus. And what I saw shocked me. This is cooking from the Dark Ages! Hot dogs, dripping in grease. Hamburgers, dripping in grease. Greasy pizza, greasier American chop suey. Starches, starches and more starches. Vegetables cooked to a mush, with all their vitamins boiled to oblivion. That's what the school department is feeding your kids. The average American child weighs four more pounds than the average child of ten years ago, and this is why. We're teaching them terrible dietary habits. Dangerous habits! And I think a basic part of good education should be good nutrition."

The audience was stirring and rumbling as she went on, and she had to raise her voice to be heard above them. But whether they were with her or against, she couldn't tell.

"Ms. Boucher?" Whittaker cut in. "Do you mind tell—"

"Bouchard," she corrected him.

"Bouchard, would you mind telling us what exactly you want, besides a thinner American child?"

"Certainly," she said, hunching her shoulders against his tone of voice. In six months she'd forgotten how a certain kind of male could use sarcasm to dominate. Six months ago, she would have backed down instantly before such bullying. But six months of freedom from Larry had made a difference. A shaft of resentment shot through her and she straightened her shoulders. "Certainly," she repeated with quiet dignity. She tipped her hat to the back of her head in a "let's get down to business" angle. "I want West Dartmouth to hire a real dietitian to plan the school lunch menus."

"*Out* of the question," Whittaker snapped. "Hiring is frozen for next year. And we have a part-time lunch director already—Mrs. Higgins. In fact, it's Mrs. Higgins that you should contact if you're concerned—"

"Oh, but I have," Kelly assured him without turning. "We spoke by phone last week. Mrs. Higgins has never taken a single college course in nutrition. She told me that she's been serving the same menu for the past thirty years and she plans to serve it for the next thirty. And that's my point exactly!" She yanked off her hat as she swept the crowd with a passionate glance.

"I'm sure Mrs. Higgins is a wonderful cook, but our knowledge of what's healthy has changed enormously in the past thirty years. There's been the Framingham report! The Bogalusa survey! The Chinese study!"

"You're recommending we hand out chopsticks in the cafeteria?" Whittaker asked nastily.

She shot him a stormy look, then turned back to the voters. "I'm recommending we limit the fat in our children's diets, as the American Heart Association has been advising for years now. I'm saying we should offer them low-fat and vegetarian meals, instead of a steady diet of red meat and lunch meats. That they should have access to a salad bar, a yogurt bar. They need more complex carbohydrates in their meals, less starch, less salt, less nitrates, less cholesterol, less saturated fats—"

She jumped as the gavel came down smartly behind her. "Thank you, Ms. Bouchard," Whittaker said wearily. "We'll take that under consideration."

Kelly pointed her hat at him. "That's not what you mean at all!"

At her back, the audience hushed.

"You're right," David Whittaker said, his voice low and silky, his gray eyes drilling into her. "That's not what I mean at all. What I really mean is that this is a commendable, worthy cause *to take up in some other year when we've got more money to spend!*" His voice dropped from a roar to a strained whisper. "So, will you please, *please* sit down and let us move on to the real business we came here tonight to discuss?"

There was no courage hat made that protected you against the disgrace of being yelled at in public. Tears of humiliation sprang to her eyes. Her mouth was ajar in a startled "O," she realized belatedly. As she shut it, she could feel a blush flooding up from her toes. With her fair complexion, she'd be glowing like a stoplight once it reached her face. Still unable to break his glare, she clapped her hat back onto her hair and tugged it down around her ears. Well, she'd tried. How was she to know she'd be facing a domineering, close-minded, pompous jerk?

"If we can get on with business?" Whittaker said in a calmer voice.

"Hey, now just a minute, Whittaker!" Leland Howard stood up. "Ms. Bouchard has brought up an extremely important issue. If we're not feeding our kids properly, then we've got to do something about it."

"Why do we have to do something about it?" A frail, white-haired old gentleman hauled himself to his feet. "Why does the darned government have to take care of every single blessed problem? Why, in my day, there weren't any school lunches! You wanted to eat, you stuck a piece of bread and a chunk of meat in your pocket and you took it to school, that's what you did! There wasn't any school bus to get you there, neither! You walked! And you appreciated it a heck of a lot more than the kids of today!"

Whittaker smacked his gavel down as three more people shot to their feet. "That's just the problem with this town!"

a motherly sort cried, ignoring the repeated cracks of the gavel. "It's full of dinosaurs like you, who've forgotten what it's like to have children! Sure it costs you some tax money to educate them. But look at it this way. You pay for them now, but they'll be paying social-security taxes to take care of you for the rest of your life, Gramps. Who's getting the better deal?"

"That's enough," said Whittaker as the woman sat. Ignoring him, "Gramps" shook his finger at the woman and tried to answer. Instead, he broke into a fit of coughing. His neighbor helped him down into his chair.

A hand caught Kelly's elbow. Startled, she swung around to find a beefy, red-faced man in a baseball cap moving her aside from the microphone. He cleared his throat.

"That's enough!" Whittaker repeated.

"Yeah, I've had enough, too," the man agreed, his voice too loud as he leaned close to the microphone. "I'm sick and tired of people telling me and my kids what to eat! What to drink! Why, my old man drank a six-pack every day of his life, ate steak for supper every night of the week, and smoked two packs a day. And he lived to be seventy-five."

"Sure, Ralph," hollered a woman by the side wall. "And from the time he was fifty, he couldn't climb a flight of stairs without wheezing himself blue in the face. You call that living, you can have it!"

While the woman and Ralph exchanged insults, Kelly looked around helplessly. There was a line of at least six people waiting for the microphone and more grim-faced people marching down the aisle to the front. Others were marching for the exits, their backs rigid with disgust.

In the confusion, no one noticed Kelly skulking back to her seat. Or so she thought, until she turned, sat and met a pair of narrowed gray eyes that blazed down at her from the dais.

David Whittaker had slumped so low in his chair his face barely showed above the table. Beneath it, he'd crossed his arms and stretched out his long legs before him. His pose spoke of infinite, disgusted weariness. Still fixed upon her, his eyes promised something more active. If looks could have killed . . .

Kelly gulped and turned down her hat brim to shut him out. How would she ever dare stand up before him to speak again? And would she ever get another chance, with some dozen people standing in line now to have their say? Somebody needed to drag the topic back to a constructive proposal. This wasn't a discussion or even a debate. It was close to a screaming match. Apparently the people of West Dartmouth did care—passionately—what their children were served at school. But seemingly no two of them agreed on the menu.

They were still going hot and heavy on the subject of food when, at ten o'clock, the custodian stumped to the head of the line and commandeered the microphone. They could argue all night if they liked, he informed them grumpily. But if they did, then they would have to shut the lights off, turn down the boiler and lock up the school themselves, because *he* was going home.

So, feeling like a chastened fifth grader, Kelly joined the crowd that trooped obediently up the aisles to the exit. But something made her look back one last time when she reached the door.

On stage, David Whittaker maintained his pose of disgusted exhaustion. But even from this distance, Kelly could have sworn that his pale eyes burned two holes through her, and her alone.

CHAPTER TWO

INSIDE HER SHOP, Kelly needed no hat for courage. Standing behind the cash register the next morning, she surveyed the room with a look of intense satisfaction. After one month of frantic effort, her health-food store, Pure and Simple, was shaping up just the way she'd planned.

The shelves were filled to overflowing with bright boxes of organic cereals and natural grains, bottles of Shoyu and Tamari and jewel-colored fruit vinegars, cartons of soy drink and carob powder and oat bran. Bins of rice and nuts tempted the eye, while pyramids of soaps made from olive oil, marigolds, sage or tuberose perfumed the air. Overhead, hanging baskets of ferns and cooking herbs gave a subtle reminder that this store was all about growing things. The breeze from a tiny electric fan near the ceiling played across a set of bronze wind chimes, stirring them to golden tinklings of sound. Her salad bar was up and running at last, and she'd found a local woman to supply her with a selection of home-baked breads that would have wrung moans of delight from a statue.

Now all she had to do was wait for the customers to discover her. Kelly's eyes swung to the bay windows that looked out on the brightly lit interior of the West Dartmouth Mall. It was a good location—that wasn't the problem. But the town had never had access to a health-food store before; her ex-husband's research had revealed that when he chose the location. It would take time to show people what they'd been missing.

"Is this dish as good as it sounds?" asked Kelly's only customer. The older woman approached the cash register, dropped a recipe card on the counter, then settled her armload of choices beside it.

Kelly lifted the card, which was imprinted with her store logo—a flourishing dandelion plant starred with yellow blossoms—and read its title. "Oh, yes, hot and spicy noodles with peanut sauce. It's one of my favorites."

The recipes had been Kelly's idea from the start. She'd been developing them, or choosing them from her favorite cookbooks, since she was twenty. When Suki was born, Kelly had stopped working in her husband's health-food store in Boston. To fill in the hours when her baby was sleeping, Kelly had taken to the kitchen. It had been her idea that Larry's customers would be more likely to buy an unfamiliar product if they knew how to use it.

She'd brought that philosophy and her recipes along with her after the divorce. Small, clear plastic boxes hung from every shelf in the store. Each box held a stack of cards featuring a recipe that used one of the ingredients on the shelf above it, and she changed the recipes weekly.

Kelly studied the foods laid out on the counter. "You'll need some fresh ginger for this recipe. Do you have that at home?"

The older woman looked guilty. "Well, I have some powdered ginger that I thought..." She paused as Kelly smiled and shook her head.

"Fresh ginger makes all the difference in the world." Stepping to a nearby shelf, Kelly selected a small tan root from a basket. "Could I give you a sample? You simply peel it and dice it very fine. Your whole kitchen will smell wonderful, and the taste..." She kissed her fingers.

Watching the woman depart with a smile, Kelly squeezed her elbows in a secret hug. That one would be back. *I can make a go of this! I know I can.* Larry had laughed when she'd told him that she meant to open her own store and that she wanted the lease to this new location as part of her property settlement. He'd predicted she'd go bankrupt in less than a year. *But I won't. I can't afford to. I have to make this work.*

She'd gone from smiles to worry in thirty seconds, she realized suddenly. That was typical. Her emotions had been riding their own private roller coaster for six months now, swooping to the heights of elation, then dropping to the pit of terror and despair, only to soar again before she could draw two breaths. That was only to be expected, her mother had assured her over the phone the previous week. She'd been reading a self-help book for new divorcées. Not that Helen Bouchard had ever been divorced—her loving husband and Kelly's father had died fifteen years ago. But Kelly's mother firmly believed that the answer to all life's problems lay between the covers of some self-help book somewhere, and since Kelly was too busy and too skeptical to read them for herself...

Smiling at the thought of her full-of-advice mother, Kelly glanced up as another customer entered the store. "Hello."

"Hi." This one looked as if she knew the difference between ginger root and ginseng. She wore a flowered T-shirt with a pair of well-worn jeans, and a thick, glossy braid hung almost to her waist. She marched off toward the shelf that held the seaweed.

With a little sigh of envy, Kelly studied her customer's hair. Larry had always wished she'd had straight hair. He thought it more "elegant," a favorite word of his. For years she'd actually had her hair straightened to please him, though the perms had dried it terribly. She shook her head, one sharp, sudden jerk that threw off thoughts of all the ways she'd tried to please that man, then reached up to touch her hair. She hadn't had it permed for six months. It was back to its old frizzy self and was growing quickly since she'd cropped the straightened ends off. It was nearly chin-length, or would be if it didn't insist on standing out from her head like a moth-eaten lion's mane. Larry would be horrified if he saw it like this.

Stop thinking about him. It's over. Done with. And she wouldn't go back if she could. To distract herself, she stretched to reach one of the hair clips she'd arranged beside the cash register to tempt impulse buyers. It was an alligator clip decorated with a marvelous assemblage of silk flowers and papier-mâché hummingbirds hovering above the blossoms on tiny wires. She'd burst out laughing when the art student had pulled them out of their box yesterday and had taken a dozen on the spot. Gathering her springing hair into a knot near the top of her head, she fastened it in place with the clip. There.

"That's, uh, awesome," her customer decided with a grin as she laid out her purchases on the counter.

"Isn't it?" Kelly shook her head to set the birds dancing and picked out the price of tofu on the register. This was going to be a nice addition to the day's take. The woman had stocked up as if she were throwing a luncheon for the Dalai Lama and all his monks.

"Hey, I know you!" the woman said as Kelly punched in the price of eight ounces of dried kelp. "You were the one who gave them what-for about the school lunches last night, weren't you? I've been meaning to say something about that for years, but I've never had the nerve."

"I don't know how I did it," Kelly admitted. "But you know, if there were two of us speaking up, it wouldn't be so hard. There was really a lot of concern, even if nobody knew exactly what they wanted. Maybe if we both stood up at the next budget meeting, and we had a list of suggest—"

But the woman was shaking her head as she dug into her shoulder bag. "It'd never work. You said it yourself—this town is living in the Dark Ages. Strictly cheeseburger mentality."

"I said the cafeteria *food* was in the Dark—"

"Oops," the woman interrupted. "Oh, darn! My wallet!" She looked up from her bag and let out an exasperated laugh. "It's not here. I didn't bring it. The paperboy came to the door to collect last night and..."

"That's okay." Kelly mustered a smile. "I do that sort of thing all the time myself." She fought down an impulse to tell the woman that she could take the stuff now and pay her later. You just couldn't run a store that way, much as she'd like to. Not with Suki depending on her.

"I'll put it all back." The woman was pink with embarrassment.

"Oh, please, don't bother. Would you like me to set it aside until you come back in?"

But it turned out the woman wouldn't be back this way for several days. Murmuring apologies, she hurried out of the store.

"Well, darn!" Kelly muttered, and started gathering up the items.

"Darn?" Victoria Ferreira, owner of Pizzazz beauty salon, which occupied the space next to Pure and Simple, struck a pose at the entrance to the shop.

"I've just been snatching defeat from the jaws of victory," Kelly told her, hoisting her armful of food as evidence. "Customer forgot her wallet."

"They will do that," Victoria agreed. "A kid told me that last month just as I was moussing her cut, after I'd spent an hour on her."

"What did you do?" Though Kelly didn't always agree with her friend's approach to life or business, she had to admit that her methods usually got results. Victoria had thrived for ten years now in the dog-eat-dog market of hairstyling.

"I picked up my scissors and promised I'd crewcut her pointy little head if she didn't phone her mother to bring the wallet *tout de suite.*"

"It worked?" Kelly laughed, trying to imagine herself brandishing a loofah sponge, or perhaps a zucchini, at a nonpaying customer.

"Her mother wasn't home," Victoria admitted. "I was afraid I was going to have to start cutting, but the little friend who'd been waiting for her tore off and raised the money from some of the other mall rats."

Like most malls, West Dartmouth had its own subculture of teens. They found the benches in its lobby the perfect place for lounging, flirting, giggling or gawking at the strange antics of the adult world.

"Probably just as well," Kelly decided. She took a tour around her friend, inspecting the style *du jour.* It must have been a slow morning at Pizzazz. Victoria had bleached a side lock snow-white in contrast to her ebony curls, then moussed the hair over her forehead to resemble a breaking wave. "I... like it," Kelly said as she completed her circle. "On you." Petite Victoria could pull it off. "On me, it would look like a tidal wave. People would run screaming for the life preservers."

"You're a statement all by yourself," Victoria assured her. "If I had your coloring or your height..."

Kelly grimaced. "You can have it!" Her height had never gained her anything but grief. She'd been this tall since she was fourteen, which had meant her stoplight head towered above every one of her classmates at an age when all a girl wanted to do was belong and blend in. And though Larry had first been attracted to her height, somewhere along the way he'd grown to loathe it. She'd given up wearing heels after their first year of marriage, but somehow that hadn't appeased him.

She squared her shoulders. "I've got to put this stuff back. Watch the front for me?" Victoria had spent the first two weeks of their acquaintance drilling into Kelly the fact that she must always keep one eye on the cash register. Kelly didn't like to think that was true, but...

"Sure, and I'll have some rabbit food, if that's okay."

"Fine," Kelly murmured, as she stacked one last item on the pizza box she was using for a tray and headed for the shelves. She and Victoria had worked out a barter system. Victoria cut Kelly's and Suki's hair. In return, she could help herself to the salad bar whenever she felt like it.

As she placed a box of falafel mix back on the shelf, she heard her friend say, "Oh, *hello!* Can I help you?"

"Just looking around, thanks," a low masculine voice replied, and Kelly's lips curved with satisfaction.

Good, let them all look. Later they'd come back to buy. She rounded the back end of an aisle and came face-to-face with David Whittaker.

He was as startled as she was. "You!" he said, his reflex smile reversing to a frown.

"Umm..." was Kelly's brilliant contribution. She clutched the pizza box to her breast in automatic defense, and a pound of tofu, two bags of rice and a few more packages slithered off onto the floor. The basmati rice burst on impact, its kernels splattering around their feet like a postwedding benediction.

Whittaker looked down at the rice, then up again. "Now why didn't I know I'd find you here?" He collected the intact packages, rose and studied his finds. He grimaced. "At least you practice what you preach." He shook his head at the tofu and replaced it on top of the pizza box.

Their eyes were almost on a level, his perhaps an inch above hers. That made him about Larry's height, another reason to dislike him. If she ever allowed a man into her life again, some time in a thousand years or so, she'd find someone tall enough not to be threatened by her own height.

Not that Whittaker was looking threatened. Perhaps it was because, though they were almost of a height, he had a breadth and solidity that made her seem frail in comparison. She looked down at his wrist as he set a bag of brown rice back on her tray. It was easily twice the thickness of hers, with a spray of black hairs peeping out from under the cuff of his blue corduroy shirt.

"You only speak when you have an audience?" he inquired pleasantly.

His irony stung, as no doubt he meant it to. "Of course not." She nodded at the package he still held. "May I have my seaweed?"

"That's what this goop is?" He wrinkled his rather hawkish nose as he studied the package, then added it to her pile. "Looks like it's gone bad in a big way. I've raised better penicillin on month-old beef stew."

She resisted the urge to tell him he looked like the beef-stew type. Probably he didn't even make it from scratch. With his impatient, very masculine, devil-take-the-hindmost air, she could see him eating beef stew from a can—cold—with a bottle of beer on the side.

Unless he has a wife. The thought popped out of nowhere, and automatically she snuck a glance at his ring finger. It was bare. She looked up to find he'd caught her looking.

His smile was neither the leer nor the sneer she would have expected. It was almost...wry. As if she'd caught him out in some failing and he was brazening it through.

Or perhaps that was her imagination. The look vanished as soon as she'd registered it. But somehow it took her irritation along with it. "The white powdery stuff is a kind of mold that adds to its nutrition. Only the very best grade of kelp has it."

This time his smile was a wholehearted grin that lighted his eyes. "You really think the kids of West Dartmouth would prefer kelp to a greasy hamburger and fries, Mrs. Bouchard?"

"Miss," she corrected. "I mean Ms."

"Ah . . ." His eyes flicked down her body in a survey so fleeting she might again have imagined it, then returned to her face. His brows twitched in puzzlement, then smoothed as if he'd found an explanation.

"Taste is a matter of education," she insisted. "And the sooner you start educating kids to eat healthily, the better."

"Taste is a matter of taste," he disagreed, "and you couldn't get that slime down the average kid with a crowbar."

Kelly bristled. "I know that! This isn't the sort of food I was suggesting you start the kids out on. But a good cook can do wonders with beans and brown rice. And tofu takes on the flavor of whatever you mix it with. You can add it to almost any dish, and its protein content—"

"Sure, I understand." Whittaker didn't look like he understood at all. "But my point last night was that this isn't the year for any frills in the budget. West Dartmouth desperately needs a new high school—it has needed one for four years."

"I understand that, and I'm all for a new high school, if it's needed, but—"

David Whittaker wasn't about to cede her the floor. "I'm sorry I gave you a hard time, Ms. Bouchard, but I don't think you understand what you did. The school committee was trying to build a political consensus last night—to get the parents fired up and behind us. That's why we called that meeting. And then you waltz in and put your foot in the middle of it, distracting everybody with your sweet little dreams of a beansprout-and-granola utopia that this town would never swallow, anyway."

He was doing it again—bullying her. Without his microphone and an audience to witness her humiliation, it wasn't quite so overwhelming, but it was daunting enough. Half of her automatically wanted to back down and respond as she'd always responded to Larry. *Yes, dear, whatever you say. If it's important to you, it must be important to me.*

The other half rejected that reflex utterly. That kind of thinking had nearly turned her inside out. For nine years she'd done everything in her power to become the elegant, sophisticated woman that Larry had wanted—and she'd failed. He'd never understood that everything that made her what she was—her love of plants and grubbing in the garden, cooking and kids, all the simple pleasures in life—were not a silly waste of time. They were the essential roots from which her personality flowered.

When he'd left her, she'd discovered herself twice betrayed. Once by him and the second time by herself. She'd sworn that she'd never back down on what she valued again. And now this man came bullying her, trying to dictate to her what was important and what was not. Kelly drew herself up to her full seventy inches and looked him straight in the eye. "Health food is *not* a frill," she proclaimed. "And low-fat cooking's an essential way of life, one we all need to accept. It makes sense—for any number of reasons. There was a study done in Bogalusa, Louisiana, a few years back. One-third of the kids showed signs of early heart disease! That's what the typical American diet is doing to our children, shortening their lives, making them—"

"Better a short happy life filled with hot dogs and hamburgers, lady, than a hundred years of torture eating junk like this!" Whittaker tapped the pizza box she held. "Tofu mozzarella pizza on rice crust—give me a break! So help me, they can take me out and shoot me before I'd eat that. Or before I'd inflict it on the poor kids of West Dartmouth. Didn't anyone ever tell you that food's supposed to be enjoyable? It's not just fuel to extend your life. Food's a sensual pleasure, right up there with sex. At its best, it's an art form."

So he wasn't quite the Philistine she'd thought. She shook her head eagerly, denying his accusation that healthy cooking had to be sterile or tasteless. If he cared about food as much as she did, then they had something in common, grounds for understanding. "Mr. Whittak—"

"What. . . is that?" he interrupted, staring at her. He shifted sideways to get a view of the back of her head, and his eyebrows shot skyward. His hand rose to hover over her hair.

Kelly felt the impact as he flicked one of her hummingbirds, setting it trembling over its flower. The straight line of Whittaker's mouth quivered, then curled upward. He batted the hummingbird again, and a laugh rippled through his voice. "I thought your hat last night was pretty strange, but *this* . . ." He shook his head. "You're in the wrong part of the country, Bouchard. You're pure California. That state's filled with people like you."

"People like me?" she asked coldly, recognizing his words as no compliment. He seemed about to flick her birds again, so she tipped her head back, putting them out of his reach.

"People who get wild-eyed and passionate about—" Whittaker looked at the shelves "—garbanzo-bean flour and—" his nose wrinkled as he read a label "—powdered goat's milk? *Yeeesh!*" His broad shoulders jerked in a shiver of disgust. "Stuff like that." He swung on his heel as his gaze roamed down the aisle. "Lord, is there anything edible in this store?" He moved a step to pick up a box. "Yeast and garlic wafers. People really eat this?" He glanced back at her incredulously.

"You're in the pet-food section!" she snapped.

"You mean people inflict this on their pets, as well? What's poor, carnivorous Bowser supposed to do when he gets hungry? Gnaw on a stick of rhubarb? What kind of sadistic nut runs a store like..." His words trailed off as Kelly tapped her chest and kept on tapping. "You? This is..."

"My store," Kelly said.

"I thought you were shopping...."

Kelly shook her head and didn't care how ridiculous he found her hair clip. "It's my store, Mr. Whittaker, and since you find it so disgusting..."

"Look, maybe I got a little carried away. It's just that—"

"No-o-o," Kelly drawled pleasantly, "you said what you think and I always appreciate that." She touched his arm to start him moving beside her toward the front of the store. Beneath the soft texture of the corduroy she felt the hard curve of muscle, and she snatched her hand away. "Unfortunately it's that kind of thinking that leads to all the overweight, unhealthy people in this country. To the polluting of our farmland by poisonous fertilizers and toxic pesticides. It's people like you who shut up calves in tiny boxes—"

"I don't have one calf in a box," Whittaker protested, starting to turn, but she caught his sleeve between her fingertips and kept him moving.

"But you eat veal, I bet, and your eggs come from chickens who've never seen the light of day, and you probably have no idea how many pounds of vegetable protein it takes to make one pound of steak," she continued as she tugged him past an openmouthed Victoria at the cash register.

"How many?" Whittaker demanded. He caught her fingers and removed them from his sleeve, but at least he kept walking.

"Ten pounds," she said, and glanced down in surprise at the fingers he now held captive. But they were at the doorway, so she wrapped up her speech. "Now, if instead, you took all that grain used to fatten livestock and fed it to the world, nobody need be hungry. There'd be enough food for all. That's the kind of perverted thinking we think in this store. But since you don't agree with that kind of thinking, Mr. Whittaker, then perhaps I can suggest the burger stand down the way?"

"After a lecture like that, it'll take a double cheeseburger to revive me," he agreed. His brows had pulled together into a dark, rumpled line, like the first glimpse of a squall forming on the horizon. His eyes had gone hailstone gray.

"Well, enjoy," she said, giving him her sweetest smile. She wanted to laugh out loud, hug herself and do a tap dance of triumph. She had actually stood up to the opinionated brute! Six months ago, she could have never done that. And it was *so* sweet!

Whittaker's eyes flicked over her face. "Thanks," he said, dropping her fingers. He reached up and batted a hummingbird, sending it swaying crazily over its silk flowers. "I'll do my best."

It wasn't a bad recovery, Kelly admitted as she glared after him. Still, on points, she'd won this round. He'd think twice before making fun of her and her store again. She turned as Victoria joined her.

"That was David Whittaker you just threw out," Victoria said.

"Yes, you know him?" Kelly agreed absently, watching as a woman shopper passed Whittaker, then glanced back at him over her shoulder.

"Uh-huh," Victoria murmured, her voice dry, her eyes also fixed on Whittaker's broad shoulders and jaunty walk. "And so should you. He's our landlord."

CHAPTER THREE

"I THOUGHT JOE ROMANO owned the mall!" Kelly moaned as the teakettle whistled. She and Victoria had retreated to the hot plate she kept behind the counter for a badly needed cup of herbal tea.

"Joe owns half the mall, and he's the operating manager," Victoria explained while she poured hot water over the tea bags in their mugs. "He decides what mix of stores they want, and he deals with the retailers. But Whittaker owns the other half. He cruises through here once every month or so. Never remembers me, no matter how much I bat my eyelashes at him." She sniffed and set the kettle aside.

"How much influence does he have with Romano?" Kelly wondered. If Whittaker disliked her store so much, was there some way he could revoke her lease? Certainly he could refuse to renew it next year!

Victoria shrugged. "Dunno. I hear they're boyhood friends. Whittaker came back from California a couple of years ago—"

"California!" Kelly choked on her first sip of chamomile tea—chosen for its soothing properties—and set the mug down. "He's from California?" Whittaker had sounded as if he'd be happy to hear the whole state had dropped into the Pacific!

"No, he's a hometown boy," Victoria said. "But he went to college out there, then stayed. He came back two years ago, and first thing anybody knew, he'd hooked up with Joe

Romano. Joe had this chunk of land. Whittaker had the know-how to design and build malls—they say that's what he was doing out West. The next thing you know—voilà—the West Dartmouth Mall, and we don't have to shop in Fall River anymore."

"Do you think he'll throw me out?" Kelly asked worriedly.

"Don't be silly," Victoria comforted her. "He's a big fish. The guy's loaded, I hear. And you're small-fry—a guppy. Why would he bother? Just because you insulted him?"

Kelly winced. "He's loaded?" Larry had cultivated a rich crowd, once his first health-food store had expanded to become an East Coast chain of stores. But the men with whom he'd played racquetball, or on whose yachts he'd raced, had been a flashier sort than Whittaker. The jogging sneakers he'd worn with his jeans today didn't fit her image of a wealthy man. Where was his gold Rolex that had to be frequently consulted in an oh-so-casual way? And Whittaker's thick hair was two weeks overdue for a cut—an unforgivable lapse in Larry's crowd. And somehow he didn't look as if he owned a car phone, or would even want to. Obnoxious as the man was, he had none of that look-at-me air Kelly associated with buckets of money.

"Yeah, he's loaded. Made it in construction work, same as his old man used to do here in West Dartmouth. And since he's been so successful, I guess he's still using his old man's methods. Like father, like son, they always say." Victoria made a cynical face.

"What do you mean, his old man's methods?" Kelly lifted her mug and inhaled the soothing, grassy scent of the tea, then took a sip.

"It was back when I was in school—I don't remember all the details," Victoria admitted. "But his dad was *connected.* All his pals were on the town council, and he was on the zoning board. There was something about a piece of swampland that belonged to the town. Right down the road from where you're living—that subdivision of tacky ranch houses, you know?"

Kelly nodded. She lived in a garage apartment in Leland Howard's backyard. It was the nicest section of town, on the river. Victoria must mean the houses downstream, where the river spread out on marshy meanders before reaching Buzzard's Bay. It was a down-at-the-mouth neighborhood, with none of the massive trees that gave her street its charm.

"Anyway, he bought it for a song from the town, though the Audubon Society was trying to get it for a bird refuge," Victoria continued. "And the next thing you know—presto change!—it's rezoned from wetlands to residential. Old Mr. Whittaker threw up a subdivision of homes before you could blink twice. He sold 'em right at the height of all the building madness we were having at the time. You could sell anything back then, especially if it had a water view. He pocketed a million from that scam, and by the time the foundations started settling and the walls cracking, it was too late. He'd worked through a dummy corporation, and the corporation had folded. Nobody could touch him. Guy was smart," Victoria finished on a note of grudging admiration.

Kelly felt no such emotion, only a vague depression settling over her like a gray, sodden blanket. That and a dull sense of...incredulity. Not that she doubted Victoria's words. Kelly herself had too recently witnessed such sharp practices in the name of the great god Profit. Why, her own husband... "But what makes you think David Whittaker is following in his father's footsteps?" she asked. Though when put that way, she thought, didn't it make sense? If that was his home training, his earliest role model...

"Well, because he's doing the political thing, and apparently his connections are as good as his dad's were. He hadn't been back in town two months when he got himself appointed to the school committee. To replace Jeanette O'Hara, who moved out of state. And guess who appointed him? One of his dad's old zoning-board buddies, who's moved up to town council.'' Victoria tipped back her flamboyant head to drain her mug, then set it down with a smack. ''Politicians, I hate 'em all!''

Kelly wasn't fond of them herself. Still, for every crooked one, there had to be hundreds of conscientious citizens. It was just a case of the bad apple spoiling things for the rest of them. ''But what advantage could he gain by serving on the school committee?'' she protested, and then it hit her.

''Well, ask yourself why he'd want to serve,'' Victoria said. ''He's not a family man—has no kids, like all the other members do. But that new school Whittaker's been pushing so hard for ever since he came back to town—just who do you think will get the contract to build that?''

''He *couldn't,*'' said Kelly, not wanting to believe that of anyone, not even David Whittaker. ''That would be a conflict of interest, wouldn't it?''

''You better believe it!'' Victoria laughed as she got up from her stool. ''But did a teensy detail like that stop his old man? You just set up a dummy corporation to bid on the contract. Then, once it's won, lo and behold, they hire our high-minded buddy, David Whittaker, to do the building, and *everybody*'s happy.'' A sardonic smile curled her pert mouth. ''Except for the other companies that bid on the contract, and maybe even bid less. And us poor jerks who pay for it with higher property taxes.'' She shrugged. ''Oh, well what you gonna do? That's the way the world goes round.'' She sauntered out from behind the counter and did a sensuous, spine-cracking stretch, her fingers laced and pointing at the ceiling.

The wet gray blanket wrapped itself tighter around Kelly. So he was no better than Larry. ''But I thought you... had the hots for him?''

"Oh, I do, I do, do I ever!" Victoria assured her. She did a little shimmy and dropped her arms. "With a bod like that, who cares if he's honest? And *rich*..." She smiled dreamily. "I wouldn't throw him out of *my* shop." She glanced at the three antique watches she wore on one wrist, then let out a squeak. "Three-fifteen! I had an appointment at three!" Her dash for the door reminded Kelly of a small breaker rushing up a beach. "Ciao, sweet!"

Kelly's smile faded as her friend disappeared. So, David Whittaker was no more honest than Larry. She drooped over the counter, her freckled hands cradling the comforting warmth of her mug. Perhaps that didn't bother Victoria, but it sure bothered her.

She attempted a smile, but it came out crooked. That was the difference between her and Victoria, she guessed. Somehow Victoria could divide her life into compartments—one for lust, another for liking, fierce loyalty to her friends in this one, admiration for a crook in that.

And Larry, come to think of it, worked the same way.

But Kelly couldn't do that, no matter how sensible that approach to life might be. Somehow she came all in one piece, rather than in boxes. She couldn't feel lust without liking, love without respect.

And she sure didn't respect dishonesty. Kelly lifted the mug, then set it down again without drinking. "Too bad," she murmured aloud, and wasn't at all sure what she was mourning. "Too bad."

AT FIVE-FORTY, Kelly's green van roared up the ramp from the mall's underground garage. Jane, the woman who worked evenings for Kelly, had come in late, due to car trouble. So now Kelly was going to be late picking up Suki at day care. "Darn, darn, darn!" she muttered.

Suki hated it when she was late. And Susan Heywood, the housewife who kept Suki and two other children along with her own daughter after school, would be no better pleased. She didn't like to start cooking her family's supper until all the day-care children were out from underfoot. "Darn!" Kelly said again. Life was so much more complicated since she'd become a single mom. And a working mom. There weren't enough hours in the day.

The driver of the car ahead of her on the road that circled the mall was in no hurry. Kelly drummed her fingers on the wheel and took a deep breath to quiet herself. She couldn't pass with evening shoppers zipping down the road toward them. She sighed and let her eyes wander to the fields surrounding the mall.

It was the only suburban mall she'd ever seen with underground parking. Above the garages, a wide sweep of winter-browned grass encircled the structure. Part of it was fenced to enclose an elaborate playground filled with cunning slides, tunnels, forts with tire swings and jungle gyms. In summer, Kelly had been told, the mall provided attendants to supervise the children there while their parents shopped. Suki could hardly wait for the warm weather so she could get out there.

For older children and adults, the rest of the space was divided into playing fields for softball or flying kites, and a park sprinkled with picnic tables. There was a wading pool that only a month ago had been a magnet for figure skaters on sunny days. It was a far cry from the acres of concrete filled with cars and sodium lights that you found at most malls. David Whittaker's idea? Kelly now wondered.

But it didn't jibe with what she'd learned about the man from Victoria. There was something generous about those playing fields; someone had recognized that people were more than shoppers.

Or so Kelly had thought. It was why she'd been so certain that this was where she wanted to open her store. But now... She sighed again. There was another way to interpret those fields. A clever man—and whatever else he was, David Whittaker was clearly that—would realize that to draw the most customers, you had to offer the best product. A mall that pleased children, as well as their parents, a mall where the men's softball team could play a game, then troop indoors for a round of beer at one of the pubs, was bound to be a success. Maybe these fields and playgrounds signified no more than that. "Too bad," she murmured, and sped up as the slowpoke ahead turned onto the highway.

By the time she reached Susan's house, it was ten to six. Suki looked like a small, blond thundercloud, and even Susan's greeting smile was strained. Babbling apologies and explanations, Kelly bundled her daughter into the van and fled.

"Sorry, Sukums," she tried again as they took a back road that edged one of the town's remaining dairy farms. She shot a glance at her daughter and smiled in spite of her guilt.

Suki was the most wondrous event of her life, a fairy-tale princess of a child. Not that Kelly could claim much credit. Suki's corn-silk hair, which would someday darken to light brown, and her incredible violet eyes, came from Larry's side of the family. But Kelly would not have had it any other way. Frizzy red curls and countless freckles were liabilities she'd not have wished on any child, much less the apple of her eye. And with any luck, Suki would top off at five foot five or so, like Larry's sister and mother. What girl wanted to be a giraffe, after all?

"I waited forever and ever," Suki fumed. "Todd's daddy was on time, and Molly's mom even came early."

"I'm sorry, sweetheart, but Jane had car trouble and that made her late. Sometimes these things happen."

"They never *used* to happen," Suki muttered, and turned to stare out the window.

Kelly bit back a sigh. No, they never used to. She'd been lucky enough to be a stay-at-home mother, and Suki had been lucky, too. That was one thing for which she'd always be grateful to Larry. He might have taken little interest in his daughter himself, but he'd furnished them with a safe and worry-free haven in the Boston suburbs. Suki had had her mother's undivided attention in those early years, when a child needed them most. It was just that those golden years made it doubly hard now to face the demands of a harsher reality.

She reached out to smooth a hand over her child's silky head and smiled with relief when Suki didn't pull away. "So how was school today?"

The sun had dropped beyond the trees by the time they pulled into their space in the garage behind Leland Howard's Victorian summer cottage. But if the sun was gone, its rosy glow lingered on and the temperature still hovered in the high forties. "Let's have a snack, then walk," Kelly said as they climbed the outside stairs to their garage apartment.

Walking held a place in Kelly's pantheon right up there with oat bran and dental floss. It was walking as much as a change in diet that had brought her and her mother's weight under control that summer after Helen's heart attack. Kelly was determined to bequeath the habit to her daughter, so that by the time she was grown, missing a walk would be as unthinkable as forgetting to brush her teeth.

"What shall we have?" she asked as they entered the kitchen. It was a cheery room, its windows overlooking their upstairs deck and the river beyond. Kelly had added her own touches of warmth—a yellow-checked cloth on the table that divided kitchen from living room, hanging baskets of basil and rosemary, rose geranium and lemon mint. The windowsills were crammed with more pots of herbs and flowers. The refrigerator door was a testament to Suki's artistic ability and Kelly's delight in off-beat cartoons.

"I don't want hummus," said Suki, coming to stand beside her and stare into the refrigerator's depths.

"All right," Kelly said with regret. "Rice with raisins and carrots?"

"Nope," Suki said. She glanced up at her mother. "Mrs. Heywood gave us potato chips for our snack."

Kelly was careful to show no reaction. "Did she?" Darn, Susan knew how Kelly felt about such junk. "Did she give you anything good to eat?"

"Apples and carrot sticks and milk."

"Well, that's okay, then." Meanwhile they were letting all the cold air out of the fridge. "Some yogurt?"

"We had that for breakfast."

"Okay, what *do* you want?"

"Frozen banana," Suki said promptly.

The bananas dipped in carob powder and sprinkled with peanuts were meant for dessert. But Kelly was in no mood to argue. "Okay, you have that and I'll still have some hummus." Later there would be chestnut soup pulled from the freezer, a salad of brown rice and greens and fruit, and a slice or two of pumpkin-pumpernickel bread topped with yogurt cheese. Kelly's stomach rolled over, sat up and waved its paws at the thought of all that. *Later,* she told it firmly. *First we walk.*

When Suki and Kelly returned from their brisk two-mile jaunt, their landlord's luxury sedan was just pulling into the driveway. They waved at its tinted windows, then stood back to let the car roll past them. Kelly noted that Stephanie, Leland's sixteen-year-old daughter, had also come home. Her red sports car gleamed in the shadows of the garage. As usual, she'd parked so close to the van that Kelly would have trouble squeezing through the driver's door in the morning. Well, that was Stephanie for you—another kind of princess altogether, as far as Kelly was concerned.

"I wanted to congratulate you on your stand last night," Leland said as he came out of the garage. "I thought you made some very good points."

"Made some points, maybe, but I sure didn't score any," Kelly said ruefully. "I'm afraid they didn't listen to me."

"Maybe the committee didn't—they're a conservative, stick-in-the-mud bunch," he agreed as he accompanied them to the stairs that led to their deck. "But you certainly stirred some interest among the parents."

"Yes." Kelly had to smile as she remembered the line of elbowing voters waiting for the microphone. "People do care what their kids eat."

Leland fixed her with his shrewd, shiny dark eyes. "So what are you going to do next?"

"Well, I… I don't know what else I *can* do." And just the thought of attending the next school-committee budget meeting and facing David Whittaker made her wince. Not that he'd let her speak again. She bet she could wave her hand in his face all night and he'd never recognize her.

"What about a petition?" Leland suggested. "If you got enough people to sign, then the school committee would have to pay attention."

"That's a thought…." Kelly hedged. It was a good thought. But she hadn't time to go house to house explaining her position and coaxing people to sign. She had a store to run and a daughter to raise.

And there was a more fundamental basis to her reluctance. It wasn't too hard for her to interact with strangers in her store, where she felt capable and in control. But out in the real world, she was almost painfully shy. It had taken every bit of her courage to speak up the other night, and she'd gotten her knuckles rapped for it. "I'll have to think about it."

"If I've learned anything, my dear, in all my years in politics, it's that the actors get things done. Thinkers just think about it," Leland said with an avuncular smile.

It was funny. Her landlord didn't look like the sort who would care about children and what they ate. And Stephanie went to some private school on the far side of town, so even if Kelly did succeed in reforming the school menus, it would not affect his daughter. Well, altruism came in all sorts of packages, Kelly reminded herself. And she'd proved to be a remarkably poor judge of character so far—witness her ex-husband. "We'll see," she said, and headed off with a wave.

She might have left it at that if, halfway through supper, Suki hadn't put down her spoon and said, "Molly buys her lunch at school every day."

"Does she, hon?" Kelly felt a thrill of dread, even as she smiled.

"Molly says only babies bring their lunches to school in a lunch box."

Hoo boy. Peer pressure, the monster that waited in ambush for every hapless parent. And each year it would just get worse, if she didn't do something to change the thinking around here. So while Kelly set out gently, delicately, but ever so firmly to refute the decree of an eight-year-old social arbiter named Molly, she was thinking fast and furiously. About how to start a petition to reform the school lunch program of West Dartmouth.

BY MORNING SHE HAD IT, and twenty-four hours later, it was in effect. "What do you think?" she asked Victoria the following Saturday morning, when the stylist dropped by Pure and Simple for a cup of raspberry tea.

Victoria pursed her mauve-painted lips as she read the display ad that Kelly had taken out in the *Dartmouth Daily*. " 'Do you care what your kids eat?' " she said, quoting the ad's headline. "That'll get their attention all right." She read further. "You want 'em to come here to sign it?"

"Where else? Everybody knows where the mall is, and they can combine it with a shopping trip. And this is the only place they'll find me."

Victoria shrugged. "Makes sense. So where's the petition?"

"Right here." Kelly brought out a clipboard from behind the counter. The petition proposed that the town hire a nutritionist to revise all school menus according to the latest guidelines of the American Heart Association. It asked that fat, cholesterol and red meat be restricted, and that a choice of meat or vegetarian meals be made available to all students. Below the text were spaces for names and addresses. Kelly had signed the first time with a flourish, and below that—

"You've had eight people sign it already?" Victoria gasped. "You haven't been open more than—"

"Excuse me?" a woman interrupted her. She nodded at the clipboard. "Is that the petition?"

By noon, Kelly had forty-three signatures. By two there were sixty-one, which was the last time Kelly had had a chance to look. She wasn't getting many chances. Every person who stopped to sign the petition stayed to chat or to scout out her store. Half of them found something to buy. Seeing the crowd in Pure and Simple caused other shoppers to wander in to see if a sale was on, and some of them stayed to buy or to sign, as well.

When Jane arrived to take the afternoon shift, Kelly decided to stay and help. Suki had gone skating with her friend Todd and his mother, so there was no hurry to rush away. Kelly was just explaining the difference between Shoyu and Tamari sauce for the fourth time when she looked up to see David Whittaker shouldering his way through the throng.

Judging from the lightning-bolt angle of his eyebrows and the jut of his chin, this was no social visit. Not for the first time, Kelly wished she could blend into a crowd. But he homed in on her like a heat-seeking missile. "Let's talk," he said, and it wasn't a suggestion.

Kelly was suddenly very glad she'd worn a hat today. As he marched her out of the store, one hand curled around her upper arm, she pulled her Red Sox baseball cap from its roll-up-your-sleeves-and-get-to-work position. Rotating the bill to the front, she snugged it down over her eyes. It was hunker-down time and let the storm rage.

CHAPTER FOUR

DAVID WHITTAKER DIDN'T explode when he stopped her under a big ficus tree outside her shop. Without letting her go, he tipped the bill of her cap up till he could see her eyes. "You've got to stop," he said evenly.

"What?" She found herself counting the beat of his pulse where it surged at the base of his throat. She could feel that beat's countersurge where his fingers ringed her flesh. Kelly swallowed, all too aware that she must keep her arm awkwardly elevated. If she let it drop, then his knuckles would brush the side of her breast and that, she knew somehow without questioning the knowledge, would be a disaster.

His lips tightened. "You've got to stop pushing that petition. This town can't handle two educational causes at the same time. You're drawing off support just when we need it the most."

"I'm not trying to hurt your campaign for a new school, Mr. Whittaker," she said, her voice trembling. "With a daughter of my own in a district school, hurting your cause is the last thing I'd want to do."

"But that's exactly what you're doing," he insisted. "You're distracting those who care about education in this town. I need them one hundred percent behind me for this bond issue, not torn in two directions. And those who don't care about education will point the finger at us all. They'll use you as another example of how education wastes everybody's money on frivolous programs, and they'll use that as their excuse to vote against the school bond."

Perhaps if his thumb had not moved across the inner softness of her arm just then, she'd have listened. But even through the cotton sleeve of her T-shirt, his touch was as electrifying as fingernails screeching across a blackboard. Who did the man think he was, holding her like an apprehended shoplifter? Telling her what she could or could not do? "Healthy food for our children is *not* a frivolous program, Mr. Whittaker! And I have sixty-one signatures so far of people who agree with me—voters," she added. She stiffened as his thumb moved again, and a red-hot shaft of sensation seared down her spine.

"Sixty—" He swore softly, and glanced toward the store. Jane was handing the clipboard to another woman. Whittaker swung back to Kelly. "Look," he said, and though his voice was quieter, it had lost none of its intensity. "You may have a point that the lunch menus need some improvement. I don't doubt you do."

Kelly's smile of triumph faded as he stroked her again. She ought to jerk free, but this was the wrong moment, now, when he was starting to agree with her. Still, that rhythmic, unconscious caress made it hard for her to concentrate on his words.

"But that doesn't change the fact that, know it or not, you're being used. You're a political red herring, Red. They're using you. Trust me."

Trust a man who'd use the need for a new school as a way to line his own pockets? She snorted. "No one's using me. I came up with this proposal myself."

"Maybe you did, but they're delighted with it."

"If anyone's trailing a herring, it's you, trying to make me feel guilty."

He shook his head. "You're new to politics in West Dartmouth. It's a bare-knuckle game around these parts, and they'll use anything—or anybody—that's handy to get their way."

Kelly raised her brows. She didn't believe in conspiracies or the faceless, wicked "they." If anyone was conspiring, it was this man.

"They'll cheer you on while you wreck my campaign, and once that's done, they'll vote down your cause, as well," he insisted.

"So what should we do?" she asked. "Give up and go home?"

"No," he said eagerly, ignoring her sarcasm. "We should stand together, that's what we should do. We should cut a deal."

The devil must be a politician, Kelly realized suddenly, silver-tongued and offering deals with a voice as soothing and sure of itself as this man's. But still she found herself asking, "What kind of a deal?"

"I'll back your cause—if you back mine," he said with a grin that could have sold swim fins to frogs.

She stiffened herself against the unexpected magic of that smile. "What's the catch?"

He looked hurt. "No catch—except that we can't put 'em both across in one year. It just isn't possible. So-o-o..."

Kelly shook her head. "No deal, Whittaker."

His smile faded. "The kids have been waiting four years for a new school. You're not first in line."

"The kids are first in line," she agreed, "and they've been chowing down on heart-hurting food since they entered first grade. Which is more important? A healthy heart, or a new school building?

"Besides," she forged on as he started to speak, "I don't agree with you that one program cancels out the other. The people in this town can be sold on both. And vegetarian cooking's so much cheaper than cooking meat-based meals—in the long run, it would save you money. So-o-o..." She jerked her arm free, then reached up to rub his touch away. "So, the answer is *no* deal. I'm not going to stop pushing for this."

"Well, you're going to stop pushing here!" he snapped.

"What?"

"Read your lease, Bouchard," he retorted. "All petitions or other political posters, events, et cetera, are to be cleared with mall management. And I can save you a trip to the office. The answer is no."

"You...you'd..." Kelly was speechless. She tore off her cap, stared at him, then smacked her thigh in frustration. "You'd do that? Where do you think we are, Whittaker? China? Bulgaria? Stalinist Russia?"

He crossed his arms. "Spare me the free-speech speech. The answer is no."

She wanted to smack him or... or stamp her feet in frustration. "You... you big... Oooh!" She slung her cap at the ceiling. It hit a branch of the ficus tree, ricocheted, and Whittaker reached up to catch it. His unthinking competence made it worse somehow—that and the fact that she was blushing her outrage and he was watching the phenomenon with openmouthed fascination. As she glared at him, he closed his mouth, but it quivered suspiciously.

"That's fine, Whittaker," she said, taking the cap he held out politely. "You just do that. And do you know what I'll do?"

"What?" he asked in a voice stiff with the effort not to laugh.

"I'll tell each and every last one of the people who come looking for that petition why they can't sign it—because David Whittaker of the school committee wants to prevent them from expressing themselves."

"Now wait just a minute," he protested, starting to frown.

But she wasn't about to wait. "Then, when I get home tonight, I'll write a letter to the *Dartmouth Daily*—no, I'll take out a half-page ad! And I'll tell the whole town what you've done to stop free speech in West Dartmouth. How does that grab you?"

Whittaker looked as if he wanted to grab *her* and give her a good shake. "No," he said, as if someone had pried the word from him.

Now it was her turn to smother a smile. *Don't like that at all, do you, Mr. Politician?* she asked him silently, her eyes widening in polite inquiry.

"That won't be necessary, Bouchard," he added stiffly. "If it means that much to you, go ahead, forget what I said. But—" he jabbed a finger at her "—don't forget this. That petition won't make one . . . bit . . . of difference. The school committee proposes the budget, and we know what we have to do. We have to ignore kooks like you and get that school built. So put *that* in your pipe and smoke it!"

She'd never met a man who'd made her so mad. A kook, that was how Whittaker saw her? Well, better that than a close-minded, pigheaded, insufferable, hypocritical—

"Do you know," he said in a milder voice, "that when you go red all over, your freckles disappear?"

Then she should stick around *him!* He was a permanent cure for the condition. Her cheeks blazed hotter with the taunt. And the smug way he'd assumed victory in this encounter wasn't helping her temper, either.

"Excuse me?"

Kelly turned to find a woman standing beside them. She hugged two shopping bags stacked to the brim with organic products. "Wow." Kelly dredged up a smile from somewhere. "You bought my whole shop!"

"Just about." The woman chuckled. "I just wanted to say thanks for opening such a wonderful store in West Dartmouth. I didn't know you were here till I read about the petition. And that's a terrific idea, too. I'm going straight home to phone my sister to tell her to get down here and sign."

"Great!" said Kelly. From the corner of her eye, she snuck a look at David Whittaker to make sure he was hearing this, and she twitched that side of her mouth at him. *See?* "Please do that. And call all your friends, too." Aware that her smirk was not in the best tradition of good sportsmanship, yet unable to banish it, Kelly turned back to Whittaker. *Take that, Mr. David Hard-nosed Whittaker!*

Her eyes collided with a subzero stare that stopped her cold. "Why, you conniving little..." There was no doubt what noun he'd have chosen. "Here I thought you were nothing but a pretty spaceshot!" He closed the gap between them—any closer and his nose would have brushed hers.

"Huh?" Kelly had seen him angry before, but nothing like this.

"You're making a profit off this, aren't you?" he snarled, jerking a thumb at her crowded shop. "You're not crazy—you're crazy like a fox! What better way to launch an unknown store than to stir up a local holy crusade—that's what's behind all your sweet concern, isn't it? You couldn't give a damn about the kids and what they eat. It's the *ka-ching, ka-ching* of the cash register you care about!"

"No," Kelly denied. "I mean, sure, it's great that they're staying to buy, but it never even occurred to me—"

"Right," he said softly, meaning no such thing. "Hey, it's free publicity, and who does it hurt? Just a few thousand kids? Cheap at the price." He flicked her shoulder. "Well, enjoy, Red."

It shouldn't have hurt, being despised by such a despicable man. It shouldn't have but, oh, did it ever. "I'm not like that!" she whispered after him as he stalked away. "I didn't even think about..."

But he couldn't hear her. Wiping the mist from her eyes, she turned back to her store. Somehow the unusual spectacle of Pure and Simple, filled to overflowing with happy shoppers, now brought her no pleasure at all.

"SO HOW MANY SIGNATURES did you get?" Kelly's mother demanded a week later. Helen Bouchard had been following events long-distance from Arizona, where she worked as cook and part-time yoga instructor at a health spa. She had gone there first as a client the winter following her heart attack, after she and Kelly had already lost some eighty pounds between them. She'd fallen in love with the place, and once she had completed her transformation, had applied for a job there.

"It topped out at 114 signatures," Kelly said.

"Well, that's not bad at all," Helen said.

"It's not good enough to make the school committee sit up and take notice," Kelly said. She glanced across the room at her daughter. Suki sat curled up on the couch, mesmerized by the copy of *Black Beauty* that they'd just checked out at the library. "Guess I was preaching to the choir. All the health-food fanatics in town came running to sign last weekend. Then it slowed way down. I'll give it a few more days, then I guess I'll mail in the petition." She didn't have the heart to go to the next budget meeting and see David Whittaker's "I told you so" smirk. He'd dismiss 114 voters as simply the town's lunatic fringe.

Or lunatics, plus one conniving shop owner. She sighed. He'd not been back since their confrontation last week, and she wouldn't have had it any other way, but still . . . "Business has sure picked up since I ran that notice. I've been advertising every week since we opened, but the petition put me on the map."

"That's wonderful, honey."

"It's wonderful, but I feel sort of crummy. I wouldn't want... anyone to think I'd just been doing this as an advertising ploy," Kelly said. Stretching the telephone cord, she moved down the counter to collect the sweet potatoes she'd been washing when the phone rang. She set them on her chopping block and picked up her knife. "I've been wondering if I should give away some of the money I've made this week to..." How did one donate money toward a new high school?

"Give it away?" Helen squawked. "Kelly, don't be silly! You can't do that. You'll be lucky if you break even this first year. Most new businesses don't. You've got to get tough now."

"You're right," Kelly admitted. Helen should know. After her husband had died, she'd opened a fried-clam shack in the small coastal town where they'd lived, north of Boston. Kelly had helped out at the clam shack every day after school. Though they'd had fun—and eaten far too many fried clams, french fries and clam cakes themselves—it had been hard work. Tough work, with no margin in their modest profits for gestures like the one Kelly was now contemplating. "You're right," she repeated, and started slicing the sweet potatoes for oven fries. She'd just have to swallow her pride and let David Whittaker think whatever he wanted to think about her.

"So what will you do if the petition doesn't do the trick?" Helen asked.

Kelly stared down at her pile of potato sticks and set down the knife. Why did everyone expect *her* to do something? She was tired—it had been a long, hectic week, and today, after leaving Jane in charge of the store, she and Suki had tackled a week's worth of chores and errands. And Leland Howard had asked her the same question not an hour before, when she and Suki had straggled home from shopping. "I'm not sure," she admitted.

"You've got to do something," her mother insisted. "It gives me the shivers to think of the way I used to eat. I wouldn't be here now talking to you if I'd kept that up."

"I know," Kelly agreed. She took an egg from the carton on the counter, cracked it and separated the white from the yolk. She dropped the yolk into a plastic container. She'd use it later to condition her hair—no use wasting what some poor chicken had strained so hard to produce.

"Maybe you're starting too big," Helen suggested. "Maybe instead of trying to change a whole school district, you should start with one school."

"Start with Suki's school?" Kelly glanced again at her daughter, but the little girl was far away, roaming the green pastures of England.

"Of course. What if you got Suki's principal on your side? And whoever cooks in her cafeteria? If you could win some converts, show 'em how easy it is to change their way of cooking, how good the food tastes, and how much money they'll save once they cut back on meat..."

"It's a thought," Kelly said as she started to beat the egg white. "That's definitely a thought." And now she needed the chili powder, the black pepper and the nonstick cookie sheet to finish these fries. "Meanwhile, do you want to talk to the Sukums?"

"You know I do."

"Don't be surprised if she neighs," Kelly warned.

With more thought and a more restful Sunday to restore her energy, Kelly decided that Helen's suggestion was a good one. By Tuesday she'd made an eleven-o'clock appointment with Mr. Tuttle, principal of Oake Elementary School.

With a name like that he'd be old and kindly, with an endearing way of peering at his students through Coke-bottle-bottom glasses, Kelly imagined. So when the secretary showed her into a large office, Kelly first assumed there'd been some mistake. This was clearly a coach sitting behind the cluttered desk.

Serving as a paperweight on the desk, a gold trophy atop which a tiny football player brandished a tiny football attested to that fact. So did the man's bull neck, meaty shoulders and his once-muscular chest that time and indulgence were converting to a soft slope down to a forty-eight-inch waistline. Lovingly displayed on the wall behind him, framed photos of a younger edition of this man surrounded by grinning members of high-school football teams also testified to where his heart really lay.

"Mr. Tuttle?" Kelly asked with a tiny prayer that she was wrong.

"Mrs...." Tuttle glanced down at a note in the middle of a pile of papers. "Mrs. Bouchard—right. Sit down, sit down. What can I do for you?"

This was going to be even harder than she'd imagined. "Er, actually it's Ms. Bouchard, and I was wondering if... I mean, I was hoping that..." She paused as a brisk knock sounded on the office door, and then it opened.

"Your secretary must have snuck out for coffee, Bill," announced David Whittaker as he entered. "So I—" He stopped short as Kelly swung in her chair to face him. "You!" he said, with more surprise then enthusiasm.

"You know Mrs. Bouchard?" Bill Tuttle asked heartily.

"Almost didn't recognize her without a hat," Whittaker said. "But, yes, we've met."

Kelly sniffed. She didn't appreciate the joke at all. She'd left her courage hat in the car by an act of sheer willpower.

"Anyway," Whittaker continued, "I just stopped by to see if you'd finished your textbook figures for us. I can come back later."

"Hey, don't do that," Tuttle exclaimed. "I've got a few questions for you. And this will only take a minute or two, right, Mrs. Bouchard?"

"Shouldn't take long," she agreed through stiff lips. That was just what she needed—to make her presentation while Whittaker sneered at her!

Instead, he turned his back as she started to stammer through her carefully planned speech. Hands in the back pockets of his jeans, he examined the photos on the wall behind Tuttle. But Kelly found his backside almost as distracting as his front. In contrast to the ex-coach, Whittaker's hips were wonderfully lean, his torso a clean, athletic wedge widening to wiry shoulders. Something about his pose made the palms of her own hands itch, as if they longed to brush those taut, denim-covered—

Horrified at where her thoughts were wandering, she snatched them back to the matter at hand, only to find herself floundering midsentence, with no end in sight. "...potato chips and...and..."

"What's wrong with potato chips?" Tuttle asked with a puzzled frown. "I eat 'em myself. Makes a nice change from taco chips."

Whittaker's head swung as he consulted something across the room. Even in profile, she could see his broad grin. She felt her own cheeks start to burn. "Well, yes, Mr. Tuttle, but they can hardly be considered a vegetable. That's like saying catsup's a vegetable."

Tuttle checked his watch. "Well, isn't it? Catsup's made from tomatoes, so what else is it gonna be? Animal? Mineral?" He laughed at his own joke. "And potato chips are made from potatoes, or I miss my guess."

"Yes, they are, but do you know how many grams of fat a one-ounce serving of potato chips has?" she asked, aware she was making no headway. It was all Whittaker's fault. He'd turned away and was now staring at the ceiling. But something in the stiffness of his pose told her he was making a major effort not to laugh out loud.

"Haven't a clue," Tuttle said with jovial boredom.

"Too many!" she snapped. "And then there's pizza, loaded with pepperoni and cheese. I've checked the menu and they serve it every week."

"Only once a week?" Tuttle laughed. "Me, I eat pizza maybe four times a week."

"Yes, I can see that," she agreed absently, racking her brains for a way to get through to him, then felt her eyes widen as she heard her own words. They seemed to hang in the air, echoing in the sudden silence.

Tuttle's dismissive grin faded slowly. "You can... Uh, what do you mean by that?" He stuck his ample chin at her, as if she were an umpire who'd just made a questionable call.

"Er, I didn't mean... I mean I just mean that..." Kelly couldn't think of one tactful line of retreat. And though it was the last place she should look—*because* it was the last place she should look—her eyes were drawn irresistibly to Tuttle's monumental beer gut.

His eyes followed her gaze, then jerked up indignantly. "You're talking about this?" He slapped himself on the stomach, setting off a billowing ground swell. "That's solid muscle, lady. You hit me with a baseball bat, and it'd bounce off. You don't believe me?"

She'd never been a good liar. "Well, I..." Kelly shook her head hopelessly. She couldn't be here. This couldn't be happening.

Whittaker had given up all pretense of ignoring them. He'd turned to watch and was grinning like a Cheshire cat over Tuttle's shoulder.

"You *don't* believe me, huh?" Tuttle erupted to his feet. "Well, come give it your best shot." He tried to draw in his stomach—it bounced chestward an inch, then sagged again. Tuttle scowled at it, then her, and thumped himself. "Your best shot, come on!"

"Mr. Tuttle, I'm sure you're in the absolutely best possible shape a man can be on a diet of meat and potatoes," Kelly babbled. *And don't forget the nightly six-pack,* added her inner voice as she hopped to her feet and retreated behind her chair. And she'd always thought of couch potatoes as a gentle lot! "I mean you seem in quite, er, reasonable shape, but that's not my point. Even people like Mr. Whittaker, who look so..." *Good* was the word that came to mind and, once lodged there, seemed to repeat itself endlessly in her brain, driving out all other possible adjectives. She stared at his flat midsection blankly, her mouth suddenly dry. "So...so fit," she managed with a major effort. "Even a person who looks that fit may have terrible heart problems and not know it, if he hasn't been watching his fat intake—"

"You're saying Whittaker's fit and I'm not?" Tuttle roared, turning to glare at Whittaker, who threw up his hands palms out in a "Hey, don't look at me" gesture. The principal whirled back to face her.

"I'm not saying that at all!" Kelly cried desperately. "I'm not making any personal judgments. I'm just saying I'd like to tour your cafeteria kitchen, maybe talk with your cooks about changing—"

"To a diet of bean sprouts and...and...spinach and grass, or whatever you weirdos eat?" Tuttle sneered, shaking his head in disgust. "You've got to be kidding, lady! Big Bertie will eat you alive if you show your face in her kitchen. And then she'll come get me, too. I'm not that crazy!"

"But this is for the good of the children," Kelly pleaded.

He shrugged, rotating his neck as if his previous fit of temper had strained his shoulders. "Guess that depends how you look at it, doesn't it?"

"It's more than just a matter of opinion! I can show you facts and figures. Recommendations from the American

Heart Association. Why, if we analyzed a typical cafeteria lunch for grams of fat—"

Tuttle turned his back on her. "Dave, what do you think?"

Whittaker's lively amusement vanished, except for a light still dancing in his eyes. He tucked his hands in his pockets and looked from Kelly to the principal and back again. "I think it's your school, Bill," he said blandly, his eyes holding Kelly's. "You're in charge."

"Right." Tuttle nodded vigorously. If he'd been a bull, he'd have pawed the floor. "I'm in charge, and so let me tell you this, Mrs. Whatever-your-name-is. Butcher? Ha—some name for a broccoli lover!"

"Ms. Bouchard," Kelly corrected him through clenched teeth.

"Oh, Bouchard, then. Let me tell you this, Mrs. Bouchard. I've got more important things to do than worry about catsup's being a vegetable or not. I've got a school to run here. And I appreciate your input, but it would never play in West Dartmouth. You show a West Dartmouth kid a...a broccoli bar or whatever you eat and he'd head for the hills. So if you don't like the way Bertie runs our cafeteria, then maybe you'd better pack your kid's lunch. How's that for an idea?" he said, advancing on her.

Kelly retreated before his oncoming belly. "That's fine for *my* child, but—"

"Good, then we don't have a problem, do we? Let him eat his broccoli bars—"

"Her!" Kelly said as he swept her out of the office. Behind him, she caught one last glimpse of Whittaker. Strangely, he wasn't smiling.

"Her," agreed Tuttle. "Let her eat broccoli bars and the other kids'll eat pizza. No problem." He slammed the door in Kelly's face.

No problem! Any school district who hired principals like that had more problems than she could ever hope to solve! Only a teeth-gritting effort of will kept her from kicking his door.

And Whittaker had been no help at all. He'd simply stood there with his hands in his pockets while Tuttle humiliated her. Suddenly the door panels blurred. She didn't need this. The last six months had been so bitterly hard, she didn't need this at all.

But need it or not, she had it. Because though plenty of people would cheer her on from the sidelines, apparently no one was going to help her fight this battle.

And it needed fighting. It really did.

So what did the little red hen always say in Suki's favorite fable? "I'll just do it myself, then," Kelly muttered. "I'll do it . . . myself." And no one, least of all David Whittaker, was going to stand in her way.

CHAPTER FIVE

"WHY CAN'T I COME?" Suki demanded, her soft bottom lip protruding dangerously.

Kelly kept walking. "Hon, how many times have you asked me that?"

"I mean it!" Suki kicked at a leaf in the gutter.

"I mean it, too," Kelly insisted. "How many times? Three? Four?" She checked her watch. They could cover another mile before turning back and still make it home by sundown. Given her eight-year-old's attitude toward baby-sitters, Kelly preferred to hand her over with a bit of the spunk walked out of her.

"Four," Suki growled.

"And what did I say each time?" Kelly's eyes feasted on a big copper beech that dominated the street ahead. They'd chosen a new route for their evening walk, past the sub-standard division built by David Whittaker's father, then over a bridge to the far bank of the river. They now walked through a section of wonderful gingerbread-trimmed homes that must have been built as summer cottages at the turn of the century.

"You said it was a school night and I couldn't stay up that late," Suki recited glumly.

"And I said you'd be bored silly. It's just a meeting about money to run the schools, hon. You'll have more fun staying home with Darlene, honest." Kelly would just as soon have stayed home herself. But though it was two days since her futile talk with Mr. Tuttle, she had lost none of her indignation. She was going to stand up and speak her mind tonight, and just let David Whittaker try to stop her.

"No, I won't," Suki protested. "I'll be boreder with Darlene. All she does is talk on the phone with her stupid old boyfriend."

"You'll be more bored with Darlene," Kelly corrected.

"That's what I said."

"Look!" Kelly cried with relief. "A rabbit. Bet you can't walk up and touch his tail!" It was a game they played. Kelly could sneak to within twenty feet of a wild rabbit. Suki's record was more like twenty yards.

"Bet I can!" Suki started her gliding creep across the lawn.

Kelly stood by the curb smiling at the tension in her daughter's small body as she moonwalked toward the unsuspecting bunny. She sucked in her breath as a pickup truck turned a bend in the road and sped toward her. *Darn.* Both hands held horizontally at waist height, she made the universal slow-down gesture. Let the driver think she was a little strange. Suki needed a victory.

Instead of slowing, the red pickup pulled to a halt. "Need something?" David Whittaker inquired as he rolled down his window.

Whatever she needed, it was not this. She felt her pulse surge at just the sight of him. "I, ah, didn't know it was you," she said. It seemed important to make that clear. "And I didn't need you to stop. Only slow down. My daughter's stalking a rabbit." She jerked her chin at Suki, who was now some fifty feet from the creature. The little girl had slowed to inch-by-inch mode, freezing each time the rabbit lifted its head.

Whittaker's brows twitched, then his gray gaze swung back to Kelly. "I thought you were a vegetarian. Or do you make an exception for rabbit stew, as long as the bunny is free-range?"

"You don't think we—" She stopped and glared at him as his grin broke from hiding. He was teasing.

"Hey, I won't tell the game warden," he assured her. "You can eat every rabbit in the neighborhood, except for mine."

"You have rabbits?" He didn't seem the type.

"Two that come dance on my back lawn every spring," he replied, his lips curling at the corners. "Always precedes a crop of baby bunnies by about a month."

A hot, sweet sensation stirred her insides as their eyes held. He wasn't being suggestive. It was just that it was spring, a time of quickening and awareness. There was a reddish haze of buds in the branches of the bare trees wherever she looked, a new something in the wind. It wasn't warm yet, but it pierced you... set you to yearning....

"So we'll leave your bunnies alone," she assured him. She turned back to watch Suki. But like a gentle hand walking its fingers up her spine, she could feel his eyes on her and she shifted restlessly. Suki had inched to within forty feet of the rabbit. This was going to be a new record.

"Would you leave something else alone for me?" Whittaker asked.

Kelly looked at him over her shoulder. She should have expected this. His warmth had just been the setup. Now here came the request.

"Would you stay away from the budget meeting tonight?" he asked, confirming her suspicions. "We've got to present the case for the new school. To get everybody revved up and behind us. We don't need any distract—" He stopped as she shook her head.

"You know I can't do that."

"You mean you won't." All warmth had drained from his voice.

"All right, I won't." She'd prepared five hundred fact sheets that she meant to hand out before the start of tonight's meeting. They analyzed the fat content of three typical cafeteria meals and compared them to the American Heart Association's recommendations. "I'm presenting my petition to the school committee tonight." It might not have enough names, but combined with the fact sheets, maybe it would make an impact.

Whittaker's eyes narrowed. "How many signatures did you get?"

Kelly gave him a mysterious smile. Why admit that, counting the last few signers who'd straggled into the shop this week, she had only 122 names on her petition? Let him sweat it for a few hours. "Plenty," she said. Plenty enough to make any *reasonable* committee pay attention.

Balling one hand into a fist, he pounded the steering wheel softly but angrily. "You're going to wreck everything."

"I don't think so," she denied. Wreck what? His hopes for a new school, or his hopes of profiting thereby?

"I don't think you care, as long as you get your publicity," he countered bitterly.

There was no way to convince him otherwise. She shrugged, putting aside the disturbing notion that she wanted—needed—to convince him, and turned back to her daughter. Suki and the rabbit stood like two garden statues. The rabbit's ears were cocked in frozen alarm.

"So, am I lucky enough to have you for a neighbor?" David Whittaker asked in an abrupt change of subject.

Kelly hunched her shoulders against the bite in those words. "We live across the river. We're renting Leland Howard's garage apartment."

"Ah . . . I should have known."

Now what did he mean by that? Kelly started to ask just as her daughter let out a wail. Ears laid back, the rabbit streaked for the bushes as if forty hounds were snapping at his cotton tail. "Suki, you almost had him!" Kelly cried, starting across the lawn to meet her. "That was tremendous!"

"I was *so* close!" Suki lamented. "I could see his whiskers wiggle!"

Kelly caught her daughter's mittened hands and swung her around in a victory twirl. "Any closer and you could have scratched his ears for him! You're the invisible girl, aren't you?"

And someone else had vanished from sight, she discovered when she looked back toward the street. Kelly stared after the truck's taillights, then shivered. "It's getting cold, hon. Want to head home?"

Two hours later, Kelly pelted down the stairs and around to the open doors of the garage. *Darn, darn, darn!* Suki's sitter had arrived only minutes ago, blithely ignoring the fact that she was twenty minutes late—which meant Kelly would be late for the meeting. There wouldn't be time to pass out her fact sheets beforehand. "Darn!" she said aloud.

Starting the van, she backed out of the garage. As she spun the wheel, she felt it shudder, resisting her turn. "Oh, no!" It couldn't be.

But it was. Her right front tire looked like a squashed doughnut when she checked it. "How could you?" The tire was practically brand-new. She kicked its treads, then stood glaring at it in frustration. Call a taxi? But the taxi would have to be sent from Fall River, fifteen miles away.

Beg a ride? But from whom? Howard wasn't home—probably was attending the very meeting Kelly was missing.

"Change the tire, Kelly," she told herself. She'd never changed a flat before, but how hard could it be? She had the van's service manual and a flashlight. "If you think a dinky little flat tire is going to stand in *my* way, David Whittaker..." She stopped short, her hand on the rear door of the van. What was she thinking—that he could have...? "No," she said softly. Not possible.

But he'd asked where she lived—asked it immediately after he learned that she meant to defy him and attend the meeting. "No," she said again. He couldn't be that underhanded. She'd simply picked up a nail somewhere, that was all. Still, she felt her jaw tighten as she glanced at her watch. Ten minutes till the meeting started.

It took her ten minutes to assemble the tools and figure out how to put the jack together. Another ten minutes to read the manual and decide where to place the jack on the undercarriage. "This is why women stay married!" she panted as she jacked up the van.

Once the wheel was off the ground, Kelly discovered that she should have loosened its nuts beforehand. The tire spun each time she turned the lug wrench. "Darn!" Could he really have done it? she wondered as she let the van back down. The garage door had been open. And her silly bluff that she had plenty of signatures might have scared him. How was he to know that "plenty" didn't mean a thousand signatures? "No," she insisted. No, she wouldn't believe that. His eyes were tough, but they met you square on.

So had Larry's.

"Bobbie! Bobbie, is that you?" hissed a girl's voice.

Kelly straightened as Suki's sitter peeped around the corner of the garage. "No, Darlene, it's me," she said pleasantly. "Who were you expecting?"

The teenager squeaked in alarm. "Mrs. Bouchard—you're, uh, you're still here!" She let out a nervous giggle.

"Yes, I am, Darlene. I have a flat." Kelly dropped her wrench on the driveway. "So I've changed my mind. I'm not going out tonight." Nor would she be going out again until she found a trustworthy sitter for Suki. Call her old-fashioned, but in Kelly's book a baby-sitter with a boyfriend in attendance was no sitter at all. "Why don't I just pay you for an hour, and you can scoot on home?"

She turned in the direction that Darlene was staring and spotted a lanky figure, hovering in the shadows of the lilac bushes near the road. "Oh, good. Looks like you'll have company to walk you back."

But watching the retreating teenagers once she'd paid Darlene, Kelly couldn't help but wonder. Had any other male crept up this driveway tonight under cover of darkness? Whittaker knew where she lived now, and the name of her store was plainly emblazoned on the side of her van. "No," she repeated.

Still, it was Whittaker's words that echoed mockingly in her mind while she finished changing the tire, then put her tools away. *Politics is a bare-knuckle game around these parts.*

Well, by luck—or by design—David Whittaker had won this round. But next round, she was taking the gloves off.

THE PROBLEM WAS SIMPLE. She needed more signatures on her petition—a lot more. And she didn't have time to get them by going house to house. So she'd have to approach her target market—the parents of West Dartmouth—en masse.

The day after her mysterious flat, Kelly delivered a letter to the *Dartmouth Daily.* She was proud of the letter, she had to admit. She'd worked on it far into the previous night, and the finished product seemed a reasonable, fact-filled but passionate call to arms for anyone who really cared about the health of West Dartmouth schoolchildren.

The letter ended with an invitation for all who agreed with Kelly's cause to meet her at Pure and Simple to sign the petition.

To her surprise and delight, the letter was printed on the paper's editorial page the following afternoon, a Saturday, under a headline that read, "School Meals Dangerous?"

"That'll do it!" Kelly crowed to Victoria.

"They sure can't ignore it," the hairdresser agreed, tapping her lime green fingernails on the countertop next to the open paper.

But apparently most of West Dartmouth could. By Sunday, Kelly had gained only forty-one more signatures. Pretty good, but not good enough.

"So they don't care," Victoria said with a shrug.

"I don't believe that." Kelly bit her lip as she scowled at the petition. "Maybe I haven't given them enough facts to convince them yet."

"Or they care, but they're lazy," her friend suggested, examining her reflection in the Plexiglas hood of the salad bar.

Kelly pulled the brown fedora she was wearing into a determined angle. "Well, if they won't come to me, then I'll just have to go to them."

WHICH WAS WHY, on Tuesday, Kelly parked beside the Dumpster at the back of Oake Elementary School. Stepping down from the van, she donned the hat she'd chosen for this occasion. Ideally she would have worn her courage hat, since this was the most terrifying task she'd ever set herself. But today she needed a hat that would attract and charm children.

The hat she'd selected was a wide-brimmed yellow straw affair with a half-size red hen made of foam rubber nesting on its crown. Two yellow chicks peeped out from under her wings. It was a confection that never failed to make Suki giggle. Kelly settled the hat into place, then went around to the van's side door to collect her willow laundry basket.

Tiptoeing up the stairs to the service entrance of the cafeteria, she surveyed the basket's contents with a mixture of weary pride and distaste. It contained some six hundred carrot-prune bars. Kelly had baked them for two nights straight, and personally, as nutritious and delicious as they were, she hoped never to encounter one again.

But they were the perfect rebuttal to Mr. Tuttle's sneer that schoolchildren would despise health food. The kids would love them. So would their mothers, Kelly was sure. In fact she was so sure, she'd included their recipe in each plastic-wrapped packet along with her rallying letter to the parents and the fact sheet that analyzed three cafeteria meals. The fourth paper in each packet was a copy of her petition that the parents could sign and mail to the school committee. Now all she had to do was pass the packaged bars out to the children and persuade them to take them home to their mothers.

"That's all," she muttered ruefully as she maneuvered herself and the heavy basket around the door and into the cafeteria.

The first thing that hit her was the noise. With their shrill voices bouncing off the concrete bricks of the cafeteria walls, 150 children made a sound like a sea-lion nursery. Kelly stopped and surveyed the rows of tables that stretched from one end of the room to the other.

The second thing that hit her was the movement—the cafeteria seemed to wriggle before her eyes, again like a beach packed flipper-to-flipper with romping seals. Children squirmed, tickled each other, tugged ponytails or traded sandwiches and secrets across the tables. Others formed a ragged conga line, bouncing from one foot to the other with joy or impatience while they waited to receive food from the cafeteria workers behind the steam tables. At the far end of the room, a tall, balding teacher surveyed the bedlam and suddenly bellowed, *"Hush!"*

The room instantly fell silent. "Row three! Go get your food now," the man bawled, sweeping the room with the ferocious stare of a Gilbert-and-Sullivan pirate.

It took a moment for Kelly to recognize this tyrant. It was Mr. Peabody, Suki's mild-mannered teacher, whom she'd met at a parent-teacher conference. As she absorbed his transformation, a row of children stood and started meekly for the end of the lunch line. Within three paces they were skipping and giggling. The level of noise rose, then surged like a returning tide. Mr. Peabody's glower changed to a bashful smile as he turned to speak to the woman teacher at his side.

Meanwhile, in the general chaos, she'd not yet been noticed. It would be just as well to pass out as many packets as she could before she had to stop and explain herself. Starting at the nearest table, Kelly smiled at the six girls seated there. "Hi, girls! My name is Kelly and I have a present for your mothers. Would you take these cookies home to her?" She passed out six packets of carrot-prune bars.

"You have a chicken on your head," a small brunette announced gravely.

"And two baby chicks," Kelly added, dipping her hat to reveal them. "See?" The children shrieked with delight. "Now please don't forget—take these straight home to your mommy."

"Wha'zis?" a skinny, freckle-faced boy asked suspiciously, as Kelly moved on to the next table and doled out another six packets.

"Cookies to take home to your mommy. And be sure you ask her to give you a piece." Kelly included the whole table of boys in her smile, then moved on while they pointed at her hat and clutched each other with glee.

Smiling, exhorting, explaining and even clucking when they started to call her the chicken lady, Kelly had almost made it to the end of the first row of tables when someone tapped her on the shoulder. "Excuse me, but what do you think you're doing?" Mr. Peabody inquired sternly.

"Mr. Peabody, I'm Kelly Bouchard, remember me?" Kelly gave him a radiant smile. "Suki's mother? We met last month when Suki entered your class." As she talked, she set the basket down on the first table of the second row. "Is Suki here, by the way?"

"She's in art," he muttered. "But what are you doing?"

She handed him a packet. "I'm asking the kids to take these home to their parents. If you'd open this and read it, it's self-explanatory."

"B-but you..." Mr. Peabody stuttered as she turned back to the table.

The first set of children had already passed her bars down both sides of the entire row. "Great!" Kelly beamed. "Good job! No, don't open it now." She tapped a dark-haired boy on the head sternly, then grinned when he turned a jam-smeared face up to hers. "That's for your mommy, honey. Take it home to her, and I bet she'll share it with you, okay?"

As she moved on, Mr. Peabody fell into step with her. "But Ms. Bouchard, you... you can't just..."

Kelly shook her finger gaily at the next set of children—a group of pretty blond girls who were clearly the class heart-breakers. "No, don't open the cookies here, girls. Take them home to your mother's, okay?"

"You can't just pass food out!" blurted Mr. Peabody, waving her letter to the parents that he'd pulled from the packet. "It could be poisoned, or—"

"Mr. Peabody." Kelly shook her head at him. "Come on, you know me! You teach my daughter. I'm going to poison her little friends in broad daylight? Before witnesses?" She tapped the bars he held in his other hand. "Here, did you read what these are made of? Grated carrots? Whole-wheat flour? Molasses, yogurt, cinnamon, prunes and just a touch of canola oil? If you're worried about poison, you'd better ask what they're putting in those cupcakes they're serving today." She nodded at a cupcake on the child's tray nearest her. "Those are loaded with heart-clogging lard. With eggs—full of cholesterol. They're made from bleached flour that's just about worthless nutritionally. And sugar's not good for kids, either."

She moved to the next table, displayed her hat on giggling demand and repeated her directions for the packets. While she did so, Mr. Peabody changed abruptly to his wrathful persona to bellow another row of children up to the lunch line. Then he tagged after her.

"But Mrs.—Ms.—Bouchard, maybe that's true, in fact I don't doubt that's true, my wife watches our cholesterol, but still..." He turned helplessly to the teacher who had joined him. "She can't just—"

"Here." Kelly took a carrot-prune bar from his hand and broke it in two. "I'll eat this, just so you'll be sure. You two try the rest." She popped her half into her mouth, made a little "mmm!" of appreciation, then moved on to the third row of tables. "These are for your mommy. Yes, it is a chicken, but not a rooster. She's a hen." Out of the corner of her eye, she saw the woman teacher hurry out the main cafeteria doors. "And see her chicks?"

"Don't you open that!" Mr. Peabody roared. Kelly jumped and glanced back along her route. Three children were looking up in wide-eyed guilt from their opened packets. Hastily they rewrapped them.

"That's right," Kelly called encouragingly. "You mustn't eat them here. They're to take home to your mommy."

"Ms. Bouchard!" Mr. Peabody almost wailed. "You *must* stop."

Kelly patted his arm. "Mr. Peabody, I do understand your concern, but I'm desperate. I wouldn't do this if I wasn't. This is a matter of life and death—it really is. And just think, any time you walk into a grocery store, you'll find a garden club or a Little League team running a bake sale. You never worry that they're passing out poison, do you? The only difference here is that I'm not selling, and I'm telling the kids to ask their mothers before they try them. Now, is that so bad?'' She doled out half a dozen more packets to small outstretched hands. ''Did you try yours yet?''

Peabody rubbed the top of his already polished pate. ''I ate a bite. It's . . . it's very good. But that's not the point!''

''What's going on here?'' The question was brought forth in a voice so robust that Kelly expected to see a man when she turned. She found herself looking down on the pink face of a woman who seemed nearly as wide as Kelly was tall. ''Just what's going on in my cafeteria!'' she demanded, brandishing a long-necked serving ladle.

''This is Bertie Higgins,'' Mr. Peabody announced, clearly relieved to be handing over responsibility. ''She's the head cook here.''

Bertie Higgins fixed him with a frigid stare. ''*And* also the Lunch Director for the town of West Dartmouth,'' she boomed, prodding him in the tie with the back of her ladle.

''Oh, yes, that too! She's the one you should be talking to.'' Mr. Peabody included them both in a wide, twitchy smile as he backed away.

''Yes, we've already talked on the phone.'' Kelly set her heavy basket on the nearest table. ''We spoke a few weeks ago about school lunches—their fat and cholesterol counts, remember?''

Bertie lifted her ladle. ''I remember I told you that everyone was perfectly happy with the meals I serve!''

''Well, actually, they're not,'' Kelly insisted, retreating outside the swing of the implement. But her step backward brought her up against a bench. ''I have a list of 163 parents in this town who aren't completely pleased with your meals, Mrs. Higgins. I mean, they are pleased, but they think—we think—that if you looked at the fat content—''

"Get out!" Mrs. Higgins rumbled. She shook her ladle at Kelly's head. "You come in here with your chicken hat and you think you'll tell *me* what to do, miss? Well, you've got another think coming! Out! Out of here!"

Mr. Peabody was one thing. This outraged tornado was quite another. "Okay, yes, okay, I'm going!" Kelly spun around. "Just let me take my—" She stopped, mouth open. The basket lay on its side, empty. Scanning the room, she could see packets in the hands of every child. They were ripping them open, discarding the fact sheets and the petition, while they popped the carrot-prune bars into their mouths.

"Oh, no!" she gasped, then looked down as a small boy tugged her sleeve.

"Mrs. Chicken Lady? Could I have another cookie? I only got one, and Jeannie took half of it."

"What are you giving them?" Mrs. Higgins yelped. She tapped the child on the shoulder with her ladle. "Why aren't you eating your cupcake, young man?" She pointed her utensil at his tray.

"'Cause...'cause I'd rather have a cookie," he whispered, squirming in his seat.

Mrs. Higgins's rosy complexion flushed to brick red as she swung back to Kelly. "You, you..." She couldn't find words to match her emotions. Instead, she advanced, her ladle out-thrust like a sword.

"I'm going!" Kelly squeaked, using the empty basket as a shield as she scuttled backward. "Really, I'm going!"

"You bet you're going, you chicken-headed hussy!" Mrs. Higgins nodded at the cafeteria doors.

Casting a glance over her shoulder, Kelly saw Mr. Tuttle, the principal, storm into the room. Two uniformed policemen tramped at his heels, and behind them trailed the woman teacher and a curious janitor.

"You're going straight to jail!" boomed Mrs. Higgins.

She was right.

CHAPTER SIX

IT WAS HORRIBLE.

Huddled in the back seat of the patrol car, her hen hat clutched on her knees, Kelly tried to tell herself it could have been worse. At least they hadn't handcuffed her.

The thought didn't help. Blinking back tears, she stared through the restraining grill at the thick neck of her driver. "What are you charging me with?" she tried for the third time, hating the way her voice shook.

"Let's wait and talk to the chief, Ms. Bouchard, okay?" His skinny companion turned to give her a bored look, then faced front again.

Tuttle had yelled something about criminal trespass and throwing the book at her. Kelly swiped at her eyes. She'd never even received a parking ticket! Why, oh why had she tried this?

The car stopped at an intersection, and she slunk down in her seat until only her eyes peeped out the window. If anyone she knew saw her... If Suki found out somehow— Oh, no, Suki! "Officer, my daughter! I have to pick her up at day care at five-thirty. Will I still be..."

The blue-shirted shoulders before her shrugged, and Kelly burst into incredulous tears. They couldn't do that—keep her from Suki! Could they?

At the station, things went from bad to worse. The chief was out at a car wreck near the mall, the dispatcher informed them as she eyed Kelly with interest. The officers looked disgusted and Kelly hung her head. Clearly they'd rather be attending a wreck than minding her.

"Please," she quavered, "don't I get a phone call?" Though who she was going to call... Her eyes overflowed again as she realized she had nobody really to call, nobody who would drop everything and come running, bringing strength and comfort. At least no one but her mother, and that wouldn't be fair, though Helen was perfectly capable of hopping on the next plane out of Phoenix. Kelly mustered a watery smile at the thought of her mother roaring to the rescue and straightened her shoulders. "Please, may I make a call?"

The dispatcher stared at Kelly's captors, and they shifted uneasily. Apparently their experience with cases like this equaled Kelly's experience with being arrested. "One call," the officer on her left decided. "At the pay phone, ma'am," he added as Kelly stepped up to the desk, expecting to be handed a phone.

Kelly gulped. "I... I left my purse in my van."

Her driver snorted and rolled his eyes. The skinny cop dug into his pants and came up with some change.

"Thanks," Kelly whispered. With shaking fingers, she dropped the coins in the slot. Leland Howard—he was the man to call.

But Leland wasn't home, his answering machine informed her with bland cheerfulness. Kelly smacked the wall in frustration, then tried to condense the afternoon's disastrous events into a coherent plea. The machine cut her off halfway through the explanation. "No!" she moaned.

The skinny cop sighed and gave her more coins. "Last chance."

As she searched the directory for the name of a lawyer, the words drummed in her head like a funeral march. Last chance. In three hours Suki would be expecting her. "Oh, *please!*" she whispered as she dialed.

Mr. Greene was out taking a deposition, a brisk female voice informed her. If she'd care to call back tomorrow...

"Thanks," Kelly murmured. Hanging up, she turned to the officers with stricken eyes.

They put her in a small, windowless room with two chairs facing each other across a battered wooden table. Kelly wasn't sure if they locked the door when they left, but she knew better than to try the knob. She was in enough trouble already.

The top of the table felt sticky. Shuddering, she pushed her chair into a corner. Folding her legs sideways on the seat, she hugged her elbows, leaned back against the wall, closed her eyes. And waited.

She tried to send her mind some place sunny, with Suki and flowers and all the grass in the world to run on. Instead her soul spiraled down into darkness—she was trapped in a place of frozen despair. More then anything, she needed a pair of strong, warm arms to hold her tight. She thought of Larry and rejected the thought immediately. He'd never really been there when she needed him. She needed...she needed...

The lock clicked, then the door swung open. Too dazed to move, she opened her eyes and saw David Whittaker stride into the room. She blinked up at him, conscious that her lashes felt spiked and sticky with tears.

"Hey..." He sank on his heels before her. Catching her wrists, he pulled her hands loose from their death grip on her elbows. "Are you okay?" Warm fingers slid down to curl around hers.

It was too much. Too much like what she'd been praying for. The fact that the comfort was coming from the last place in the world she'd have expected was the final straw. Her eyes filled. "No..." She tried to smile. "Not really. I mean, I've been better...."

His smile came slowly, reminding her of the flame in a lamp as the wick is turned higher. "I can see that." He squeezed her fingers. "You ready to go?"

"You're t-taking me out of here?" she asked incredulously. He should be enjoying her humiliation. Instead, he was rescuing her? "Why?"

His smile went faintly lopsided, but the irony seemed directed inward. "Because I can picture you anywhere but here?" He spoke as if he were testing the words, searching them for an unexpected truth. He shrugged, then stood with an easy, muscular grace, still holding her hands. "Ready?"

He pulled a red bandanna from his back pocket and handed it to her. As she blew her nose, she noticed he was wearing well-worn jeans today, with a smear of dirt on one knee.

His eyes followed hers. "I was out in the garden when Bill Tuttle called."

And he hadn't bothered to change. He'd come running. She tried to swallow and found something sharp in her throat. "Are you paying my...my bail?" she muttered while they walked down the corridor.

"Nope. Bill dropped the charges." His pace quickened, and the grip on her elbow tightened slightly.

If the school principal had dropped the charges, then Kelly knew who had made him do it. But why?

They stepped into the front room and she flinched as the eyes of half a dozen police officers swung her way. A rail-thin, graying man in a rumpled business suit pushed away from the wall and started toward her. "Ms. Bouchard? I'm Elliot Freeling of the *Daily*—"

"Not now, Elliot, give her a break," Whittaker cut in, putting up a hand to fend off his advance. He curved an arm around Kelly's shoulders and swept her toward the exit. "Ms. Bouchard's had enough for one day."

"Just a question or two?" insisted Freeling.

"Sorry."

Kelly glanced back. Freeling had followed them outside. "I'll be in touch, Ms. Bouchard," he promised, lifting his pen in farewell.

Whittaker swore under his breath and hurried her around his pickup. As he opened her door, Kelly flinched at the sight of her chicken hat lying on the seat, then was practically lifted into the vehicle.

"Who was that?" she asked when he slid in beside her.

He didn't look her way as he steered the truck out onto the road. "Freeling's editor of the *Dartmouth Daily.*" His voice sharpened as she looked back at the journalist's diminishing figure. "I didn't think you'd want any more...attention than you've had already."

Half of her agreed and was deeply comforted by his consideration. But a tiny warning bell chimed in the other half. Once she would have taken a man's motives at his word. But after Larry... "No, publicity's the last thing I want," she said, then couldn't resist adding, "in spite of what you think."

The corner of his mouth curled. "I've given up on that theory. Nobody would go through this much grief just to publicize a store."

Thank heavens he'd realized that, at least!

"No," he went on, "I've gone back to my original impression." As they flicked her way, his eyes sparkled with laughter. Guessing the verdict, she lifted her chin defiantly. "You're a loose cannon in a chicken hat," he concluded, blithely mixing his metaphors. "A do-gooding spaceshot."

"I am not!"

"Not that that can't be dangerous," he added, ignoring her denial. "And one hell of a nuisance."

That she couldn't deny. Not after this. "So, go ahead. Laugh."

"Not today, Kelly." Gray eyes fixed on the road, he brushed her arm with the back of his knuckles, then concentrated on his driving.

With a grateful sigh she accepted the temporary truce and closed her eyes. Then it hit her—he'd used her first name. A flush of warmth spread out from her center in slow ripples.

She opened her eyes when the truck stopped to let a car turn across the traffic. "Where are we going?" she asked in sudden alarm.

"I'm taking you home."

It took her a second to translate that—he meant her home, of course. For a silly second she'd pictured someplace else, one of those old homes on the far side of the river, with a garden in the backyard where rabbits danced in springtime. "I don't want to go home. My van's at the school." She shuddered, thinking of her return to the scene of her humiliation.

"All right." He flipped the truck's turn signal.

"Thank you," she said softly. "In fact, thank you for everything."

"Thank you, *David,*" he amended just as softly. His lips quirked when she shot him a troubled glance. "And don't say we don't know each other well enough. If I'm going to have to spring you from jail every time I turn around—"

She shuddered. "Don't!"

"Okay," he agreed peaceably.

They made the rest of the trip in silence. As they drove around the side of the school, Kelly reached for her hat, then thought better of it. Beside her, David's breath puffed out in a silent laugh. "Maybe not," he agreed. "But my sunglasses are in the glove compartment if you'd like to—"

"No, thanks," she muttered. So he knew why she wore hats. She didn't know if that made her feel comforted or threatened. The latter, she decided, then forgot it as they approached the back of the building, by the cafeteria. "My van! I left it right beside the Dumpster!"

David swore under his breath. "I'll go find out. Wait here."

Panic rising, Kelly checked her watch as he left. Thirty minutes until Suki expected her. She clasped her hands to stop their trembling.

When he returned, David's face was grim. He swung in beside her, started the engine, then caught her hand in a quick squeeze. "He had it towed," he said briefly. His jaw tightened as she emitted a wordless yelp of anguish. "You've got to understand, Kelly. Bill Tuttle's an ex-football coach. He operates on different rules. You hit your opponent hard enough to knock him down and keep him down. That's just the way he thinks."

"But I *need* that van!"

"I've taken care of it. It'll be delivered to you first thing tomorrow. The tow lot's closed now. It's after five."

"But I need it *now!* I have to pick up Suki at day care!" Her voice wobbled dangerously. This was one blow too many.

David stopped the truck. "Hey... easy." He touched her chin. "No problem. Just tell me where."

Funny that a touch could pierce her the way this one did. She blinked frantically, fighting back the tears. Or perhaps it was his strange, pale eyes that pierced her with such terrifying ease. They seemed darker now, their pupils like widening targets at the center of his blue-rimmed irises. She shuddered and twisted away, just as his fingertip brushed her bottom lip. Her breathing staggered in her chest, and she couldn't have said how long they'd held that look. It might have been only seconds, though it had felt like hours. "It's... it's on Wilkes Dairy Road. Number twenty-three."

"Fine." His voice sounded strange, but then, everything seemed strange this afternoon. She just wanted to go home and hide.

When they reached Susan Heywood's house, David waited in the car while she went to collect her daughter. Kelly breathed a sigh of heartfelt relief when Suki looked up from a picture puzzle with her usual squeak of joy. Clearly she'd not heard about her mother's misadventure. Kelly knelt and swept her into a passionate hug. *Oh, thank you, thank you!* she thought, brushing her cheek through Suki's wondrous hair. "Oh, Sukums!" If Suki had been scared, she never would have forgiven herself.

Suki backed out of her arms to study her, her brows crinkled into a puzzled frown. "You okay, Mommy?"

Kelly forced a smile. "I'm fine, honey. Just a hard day."

They left Susan's house hand in hand, Suki chattering about her day, but as David stepped down from his pickup she hushed. He preceded them around the vehicle to the passenger side and opened the door. "Where's our van?" Suki demanded, looking up at her mother.

"I parked it in the wrong place and it was towed," Kelly explained hurriedly. "So, Mr. Whittaker is giving us a ride."

"But you can call me David," he added as Suki looked from him to the high seat of the truck. "Can I help you up, Suki?"

"I'll do it," Kelly insisted, but David had already held out his hands, and Suki stepped into them without a protest.

"*Up* you go, big girl!" He set her on the seat, then placed the hat in her lap. "And you get the chicken." Suki patted the bird, then scooted over to snuggle against Kelly as she settled on the seat beside her.

They rode for a while without talking. Suki's normal chatter was silenced by her shyness around strangers, and Kelly was tongue-tied by emotional exhaustion. It was David who finally spoke. "Could I take you two out for pizza, Kelly? You don't want to worry about cooking tonight."

Grateful as she was to him for his rescue, the last thing she wanted—tonight or any night—was to sit across a table from the school-committee man and grope for topics of conversation. "No, thank you, David." She just wanted to go home, hole up with Suki, eat some real comfort food, then stagger into bed and wipe out this day with sleep. She had a nut-and-tofu loaf in the freezer that tasted better than any meat loaf. That would do, she decided.

"Mommy doesn't feel good," Suki explained. "She had a hard day."

"She sure did," David agreed. "So what's your advice, Suki? What do you do when you want to cheer up your mother?"

Kelly shot him a resentful glance—he talked as if she was collapsed in the back of the truck, rather than sitting here within arm's length. But he and Suki were exchanging a considering look.

"Well, I hug her," Suki told him. "Like this!" She slid her small arms around Kelly's waist and gave her a hearty squeeze.

"Sounds like a good idea," David agreed, laughter shimmering behind his words. "What else cheers her up?"

Suki frowned, then brightened. "We go for a good, long walk."

"She might be too beat for that tonight," David warned. "Besides, I think she missed her lunch."

"She is," Kelly said tartly, "and she did. And if you two don't mind..."

"Well, we'll eat supper then," Suki said with decision. "And then she should take a bubble bath, with lots of candles around the tub the way she likes them, and some pretty music playing...."

"She likes that, does she?" David asked softly. He nodded to himself. "Sounds like just the ticket."

Kelly felt her cheeks burn. Suki had opened the door on their private world. For a second she felt as if she and David shared the same mental image—of her, breast-deep in bubbles, her damp hair knotted on top of her head. And of David, stopped short in her bathroom doorway, his eyes wide with wonder in the flickering candlelight. A shiver twisted across her shoulders. "Well, now that you two have planned my evening for me . . ." she growled. But Suki was right. A bubble bath sounded heavenly.

When David pulled the truck into her driveway, Kelly gathered the last of her energy. She slid out her door, then lifted Suki to the ground and handed her the keys. "Run on up, hon. I'll be right behind you."

With a wave to David, Suki scampered out of sight, and Kelly stopped at his window. How could she tell him what his support had meant to her today? Words couldn't express it. A touch might have, but since that road was closed . . . "Thank you," she said, and was appalled at how inadequate it sounded.

"No need," he said quietly.

His gaze was like a path of light between them, a path she didn't choose to follow, but whose existence she couldn't deny, however much she wished to. She wanted no connection with this man, no matter how decent he'd been today. "Thank you," she said again, and turned away.

Once she'd started moving, it was easier to widen the gap between them. She hurried up the stairs to the deck, then paused, not knowing why she waited. David's headlights swept slowly across the yard, then left it once more in darkness as his truck purred off into the night. With a heavy sigh, Kelly went inside.

She and Suki had just finished supper when a knock sounded on the door. Kelly looked down at the floor-length, white terry-cloth robe she'd donned before cooking and grimaced. The last thing she wanted was a visitor. Her whole body ached with tension, and she was longing for that bath she'd promised herself. She padded to the door, drawing the belt of her robe tighter around her waist.

David stood on the deck, a white shopping bag dangling by his side. "Sorry to disturb you again, but I thought this might come in handy." He handed her the bag, his eyes flicking over her robe. "I see I caught you in time."

To do what? she wondered, looking down at the bag. It was imprinted with the logo of an exclusive department store at the mall where Pure and Simple was located. But if this was a gift, she didn't want it. She owed him too much already, and gratitude was a string that tied the receiver to the giver. Just standing there, she already felt as if invisible skeins of emotion linked them together, like those silken, silvery threads a spider spins in the garden at dawn. "What is . . . ?"

As a pair of heavy feet clumped up her stairs, she turned in relief. Leland Howard's face rose into view, a look of surprise growing on it as he spotted David. "Kelly, I just played my phone messages," he said as he reached the deck. "Do you mean to tell me they arrested you?"

"Not exactly," David cut in. Swiftly he outlined the day's events. As he spoke, Kelly felt her cheeks burn. If this tale had to be told, then it should be she who told it. David's bald accounting left out the reasons she'd acted the way she had, made her sound even more the fool.

But she needn't have worried. Her landlord was on her side. "Why, that's absurd!" he burst out when David had finished. "Calling the police down on a parent! Tuttle's a bull in a china shop—no sense of proportion. I've a good mind to call him before the town council to explain himself. This is outrageous!"

"I've already apologized to Kelly," David said dryly. "And as for Tuttle, the school committee can handle it, Leland. Don't worry about it."

Leland bristled. "I certainly will worry about it when a concerned parent is harassed and bullied, simply for showing her concern!"

The muscles in David's jaw bunched. "It wasn't a case of bullying. There was a misunderstanding, and it has been cleared up. End of story."

Kelly felt her spine stiffen. Bill Tuttle certainly *had* bullied her, with his threats of pressing charges. Now David was brushing the painful incident aside as if it was nothing.

"Maybe it is, and maybe it isn't," Leland allowed. "Even if we don't call Tuttle up for a hearing, I'm not about to drop it here."

"Fine. Don't then." David crossed his arms. "Meanwhile, Kelly and I were having a conversation. . . ."

"Oh?" Leland's eyes shifted from David to her and back again. "Oh."

Oh, what? Kelly felt a flash of annoyance, at David for the high-handed way he was routing Leland from her doorstep, and at her landlord, for whatever conclusion he was leaping to. She opened her mouth to countermand David's statement, then shut it again. She had no desire for Leland's company tonight, after all. "Thanks for coming over, Leland," she said as he made a move toward the stairs. "I hope my message didn't alarm you."

"Oh, not at all, not at all." Her landlord shifted from one foot to the other. He looked as if he didn't like to leave them together. "I want to hear more about the incident when you have time to talk."

"Certainly," Kelly said, though she'd just as soon forget the fiasco. "Stop in tomorrow for a cup of tea, if you like."

"I'll do that," he promised, while David scowled. "Good night, then, Kelly," he added, pointedly omitting David from his farewell.

When he'd gone back down the stairs, David let out a breath between his teeth. "He's using you," he warned softly.

"He's a perfectly nice man, and I'd like to drop this," Kelly retorted. She didn't know who to believe anymore, and she hated the feeling. She'd come to this town to get her feet back on the ground. To devote herself to the pure and simple pleasures in life. Instead, she'd stumbled into the middle of this... this range war, and she didn't even know who wore the white hats. "And I'd also like to say good-night, David."

She caught the doorknob and started to back into her apartment, but his hand closed over her fingers. "Kelly, this isn't the time, but we need to talk. I was planning to see you, anyway, before this happened today. I've been out of town this weekend or I'd have contacted you sooner."

"About?" She was so tired her knees were shaking. She tried to pull back, but his grip tightened warmly.

"About the usual. That letter of yours in the paper on Saturday, and now this. I want you to promise me something—if Elliot Freeling calls, don't talk to him. Not until we've had a chance to talk. Would you do that for me?"

And the final piece in the awful jigsaw of the day's events fell into place. David hadn't come running just because she needed a friend, had he? That wasn't how people operated in this world, no matter how much Kelly wanted or needed to believe it. He'd come to help her because she could still hurt him and his campaign for the new school if he didn't.

He'd feared distracting publicity from the start, she realized. So what could hurt his campaign more than an article about Kelly and her cause in the local newspaper? An article made all the more newsworthy by Kelly's brush with the law. "So that's where the string's attached," she said softly.

His head jerked up. "What are you talking about?"

"That's why you helped me today—so I wouldn't talk to the paper, isn't it? I may have looked like a loose cannon, but Tuttle looks like a bully. That makes you all look bad."

"Now just a damned minute!" David started to pull open the door.

"No! Please don't." She put a hand on his chest to stop his advance. "I've had enough, David. I don't want to talk about it."

Scowling, he paused. His eyes swept down to her restraining hand, then back to her face.

"I *mean* it, David!"

"All right." He let out a hiss of frustration. "You've got it all wrong, but all right. I see your point for tonight. We'll talk about this later."

"Thank you." Backing inside, she closed the door between them.

"Just don't answer your phone tonight if you don't want to talk about this to Freeling!" he called through the paneling.

That was good advice, she realized. She'd unplug the phone and shut out the whole blasted world.

But as David's truck purred out of her driveway, she realized that she still held his package. The bag contained an enormous, velvety bath towel of midnight blue, two long white beeswax candles, and a box of lily-of-the-valley bubble bath. With a bewildered laugh, she set David's gifts out on the table, and then found one more. He'd included a cassette that, from the worn condition of its case, had clearly been played many times before. It was a recording of the hauntingly beautiful song of the humpback whales. "You're a strange man, David Whittaker!" she whispered. But as she went off to take her bath, she was smiling again.

CHAPTER SEVEN

THE NEXT MORNING David drove up in Kelly's van just as she was waving Suki off on the school bus. "Morning," he said as he rolled down the window. "Feeling better?"

"Yes." His lily-of-the-valley bubble bath had washed more than her blues away last night. She'd scrubbed away her anger at David, as well. So, he'd had his own hidden agenda for removing her from jail and Elliot Freeling's attention. Still she couldn't really fault him for acting in his own interest. People did that everywhere, everyday. She just had to remember not to take his kindnesses seriously. "I loved the whale songs."

"Thought you might," he said with the easy warmth that made him so attractive.

"And the candles," she added quickly, "and the..." Somehow, she didn't want to mention the bubble bath or the towel. "And the other things."

"I'm glad," he said simply, then patted the side of her van. "Would you have time to drive me back to my car?"

"Of course. Let me get my purse."

"And I wanted to talk to you about Freeling," David added as they pulled out onto the road a few minutes later.

The man never let up, did he? Kelly sighed. "Must we?"

David nodded. "I don't think you begin to understand the damage you could do here, or the political undercurrents. But maybe if I explained."

She shrugged. He had a captive audience, after all.

"When I was growing up in this town," he continued, "we had one of the finest high schools in southeastern Massachusetts. So I was shocked, when I came back, to find how much that had changed. The town's not been spending the money on education it should have. The high school's old and out-of-date. So's the junior high. As a result of that neglect, the parents with money have pulled their kids out of the public schools. Sent them off to private ones, where they'll get proper schooling."

Kelly shifted restlessly. Howard's daughter Stephanie attended a private school, but...

"So that means the most influential people in town no longer have a stake in the public schools," David went on. "It doesn't affect their kids. And since they're paying private tuition already, they're not willing to pay higher taxes to improve the public schools. That's where Howard and his buddies are coming from. And that's where Howard makes political hay."

Perhaps this was true, but why did David care? As a rich, childless, single man, he ought to be siding with Howard's crowd—if such a clique really existed outside David's imagination.

"That's the main faction that opposes the high school," David said. "Against them you've got the parents of the kids, mostly middle-class folks, busy making a living. The opposition's been better organized these past four years. But this year we thought we could put together a coalition to finally pass the building bond. Until you barged in..."

Kelly shook her head in protest. This was where she didn't agree.

"That's why I don't want you talking to Freeling," David insisted. "He's on the other side. There's something gone sour about the man, some bitterness that comes out in his editorials." He waved a waiting car into the road ahead of them. "Anyway, all I'm saying is, please, consider before you give Freeling an interview. You made yourself a heck of a news item yesterday. Don't let them make you a martyr, unless—" his eyes narrowed "—that's what you want."

Kelly sighed and rested her head against the seat back. "I don't accept that our causes cancel each other out. That's where you're wrong." Startled, she opened her eyes as he thumped the steering wheel.

"*Dammit,* Kelly! We don't have the money for a nutritionist! We just don't have it! And if we did, what would you want us to do? Fire Bertie Higgins? She's run the school lunch program for the past thirty years."

Picturing that ladle-wielding terror, Kelly grimaced. Still, he had a point. You don't discard people just because they're a little dated. But Mrs. Higgins reminded her of her own mother back in their clam-shack days. Her kind of cooking was clearly as harmful to herself as it was to the children. People had to change with the times, accept and use knowledge as it was acquired. How else was life to be improved?

David claimed her attention again. "So, since that's the case, what would make you happy?" he demanded.

Happy? It had been quite a while since she'd felt that emotion. Oh, the simple pleasures of life with Suki—the cooking, the rabbit-sightings, their walks and play brought her peace and contentment. But when had she last felt that all-encompassing joy that buoyed you up and carried you through life the way a river carries a swan? "Happy?" she echoed, her eyes focusing gradually on his profile etched sharply against the sunshine. A thought stirred—a thought so wistful, so idiotic, that she brushed it aside before it could unfold its bright wings and reveal itself.

"Happy," David repeated, frowning. "What could we do to improve the menus that would cost us nothing?"

And shut me up, Kelly added ruefully. Here she'd been thinking about her life, and he was just trying to make a deal. "Where's the free lunch?" she asked. "I don't know. Most improvements take money."

"Haven't got it, I tell you. There must be something else."

"Well..." Kelly frowned, trying to think. "The actual preparation of the food makes a huge difference, as well as its contents—what kind of cooking oil Mrs. Higgins is using, whether she's deep-frying or broiling, whether she cooks with whole or skim milk. I couldn't say if her methods could be improved on the cheap without watching her cook."

"That's no problem," David said crisply. "If you want to watch her cook, I'll get you in there."

"Umm..." The last thing she wanted to do was walk into that cafeteria again. She'd been such a fool to try that stunt yesterday. Larry had often accused her of leaping before looking, but even for her, that had been a whopper.

But whatever her personal humiliation, nothing had changed for the kids. They were still being served meals that would steal years from their lives. To go back in there would be excruciating, but if she really could make some suggestions that would improve the meals... If David really did have the clout to make Mrs. Higgins accept her advice...

The van had stopped at their destination. David put a fingertip to her jaw and turned her face to his. "Well?" he demanded.

The rhythm of her breathing tripped, then steadied as his hand dropped away. She took a deeper breath. "I think... okay—if you'll be there."

His eyes warmed. "If you like, sure."

"To protect me from Mrs. Higgins," Kelly added quickly. "That woman terrifies me."

"Ah." His face hardened subtly. "Yes. She terrifies everyone. But she's got a heart of gold, Kelly, once you get to know her."

"I'm sure," Kelly agreed, not sure at all. She took another deep breath and was suddenly conscious of the lift of her breasts as she did so. "Okay. We'll do it. When?"

"Tomorrow," David said promptly. "I'll call Tuttle soon as I get home."

AS SHE ENTERED Oake Elementary School the next morning, Kelly caught a glimpse of herself in the glass doors. She'd worn her dress-for-success suit—a tan linen blazer and skirt, which she'd combined with a forest-green silk shirt and a pair of low heels. She'd pulled her hair back in a severe chignon, and her only jewelry was a pair of gold ear studs. *And no hat,* she thought grimly. Let Tuttle dare object to this ensemble.

Her eyes swept the lobby and found David just as he turned away from a trophy case. His brows jumped, then he crossed to meet her, a smile slowly dawning. "Very nice," he applauded, his pale eyes making a rapid but thorough transit down her leggy length and up again. "Responsible. Serious, but not too earnest. Competent, yet not overly aggressive—" his lips twitched wickedly "—and no chickens."

"Pig," she enunciated with sweet precision, and headed for the principal's office.

Laughing, David caught her arm. "Bill says he doesn't want an apology, Kelly. He's sulking today, so let's just let him be, shall we?"

"Sulking? What for?" she asked, as David led her down a corridor.

"Bertie Higgins had a whole litter of kittens in his office when he told her you're to have free run of her kitchen. And then Leland Howard dropped by to yell at him. I expect he wishes he'd never heard of you."

"Oh, dear." She'd meant to make her peace with Bill Tuttle if it killed her. Now she wondered if their feud was past mending.

"He'll get over it." David glanced at her sideways, then shook his head. "That's quite a disguise," he noted admiringly. "You don't look like the same woman."

She didn't look like her usual fey and dithery self, he meant. Kelly sniffed, wondering where he'd acquired his low opinion of alternative life-styles. California, no doubt, she decided as they pushed through the cafeteria doors.

The room was silent and empty, its lights dimmed so that the only spot of brightness was the long serving window that opened into the kitchen beyond. A teacher stood silhouetted at the counter, filling a foam cup from a coffee urn. She dropped a coin into a bowl, then turned. "Mr. Whittaker! Hel*lo*." Her smile graduated from politeness to eager warmth. Her eyes appraised Kelly as she raised her cup of coffee and sipped. "Ugh!" She stared down at her beverage in horror. "That's...that's disgusting!" She set the cup back on the counter. "Don't risk it," she advised. "Bertie's on the warpath about something."

Kelly could guess what as David slanted her a knowing smirk, then drew her into the kitchen. "Courage, my friend," he murmured.

He was enjoying himself, she realized, and would have shaken off his arm—except that Bertie Higgins was eyeing her from the far side of the room. As the cook peered through the welter of pots and utensils that hung from a beam between them, she reminded Kelly of a rhino, squinting through the brush while it debated a charge. Kelly sucked in a deep breath and moved forward on her own. "Mrs. Higgins," she said, holding out her hand, "it's so nice of you to let me visit your kitchen."

Bertie Higgins's eyebrows shot up above her deep-set blue eyes. Her florid complexion went a shade pinker across her snub nose and cheeks as she stared at Kelly's outstretched hand. "You think so?" she countered.

With her hand dangling in midair, Kelly forgot the apology she'd prepared. "Well, I appreciate it," she said faintly.

"Do you? Then stay out of our way. We've got a lunch to put out." Mrs. Higgins steamed past her, donned oven mitts and yanked open the glass doors of a big commercial oven.

Timidly Kelly followed to peer over the cook's shoulder. The oven shelves were stacked with trays on which pieces of fried chicken sizzled. Each piece sat in its own puddle of drippings, and the batter gleamed with more grease. "That's what I mean," Kelly said softly as David drifted up beside her. When Mrs. Higgins turned to glare, she added, "I suppose you buy the chicken prefried, then you reheat it here?"

The cook gave her a majestic nod.

"And the skin is still on the pieces?" Kelly added.

This nod was tighter. The cook sailed away to berate a small blond woman who was stirring something in a large kettle on a stove top.

"This isn't a heart-healthy meal," Kelly told David flatly. "Chicken skin's full of fat, and when you batter and fry it, you double the fat count."

"What could she do to improve it?" David asked.

Kelly shrugged. "It shouldn't be fried at all, and the skin should be removed. But I doubt if you can buy it skinned, and she hasn't time to skin chicken for three hundred children. I'd throw out this recipe and substitute turkey, or something vegetarian."

"*Vegetarian!*" Mrs. Higgins snorted, popping up at Kelly's elbow. She opened the door to a massive steam cabinet. As steam billowed out, she gestured at a tub of gray-green, mushy-looking string beans, which floated in a buttery sheen. "The kids hate vegetables! Just check their trays at the end of this meal. If you fed them nothing but veggies for lunch, they'd lie down and starve before they'd eat them. Take my word for it."

"She's got a point," David allowed as she stormed off. "I remember in third grade a buddy and I collected all the beans at our table. We'd created a six-foot mural of bean porcupines under bean pine trees, with bean grass underfoot before they hauled us off to the principal."

She could just picture him in third grade, brash and bright-eyed and full of mischief. She smiled in spite of herself and turned away to watch Bertie Higgins shove a pan of mashed potatoes into the oven. "Instant mashed potatoes?" she asked the woman, who merely grunted in agreement. Kelly kept her polite smile plastered in place. "Would you mind my asking what you put in the recipe?"

"Yes," the cook said, and wiped her surprisingly small and delicate hands on her stained apron.

"Now, Bertie," David drawled on a note that was halfway between teasing and warning.

"Don't you now *me,* David Whittaker!" she snapped. "I remember you when your eyes hardly peeped above the tray rails. And the time you brought that frog in here and tried to put it in the soup."

"It was a toad actually," David admitted. To Kelly's delight, the tips of his ears reddened, and he jammed his hands into the pockets of his trousers. "But what's in the potatoes?" he persisted.

"What any fool puts in mashed potatoes—salt, pepper, butter, whole milk, a touch of half-and-half to make 'em rich. But I suppose Miss Nitpicker here will find something wrong with that, won't she?" Bustling off, the cook began pulling the chicken out of the oven.

Across the room another cook was unloading pans of sheet cake from a pastry oven, while a second worker brought forth cups of pallid fruit cocktail from a restaurant-style refrigerator. The tempo in the room was increasing. The far wall was patterned with an ancient, abstractly beautiful pattern of grease smoke. A large black clock pointed its hands to eleven-fifteen. The first lunch shift would soon be arriving.

"I'm afraid she's right," Kelly said, her lips close to David's ear to be heard above the roar of the overhead exhaust fans. "She should use skim milk—not whole, and certainly not half-and-half. And since she's giving the kids gravy, she could cut out the butter altogether."

She frowned at a vat of brown gravy swirled with a film of grease. "Better yet, forget mashed potatoes and simply make oven fries with the skin left on. All you have to do is slice them, spray them with a smidgen of olive oil, shake them in a bag with some paprika or oregano, then bake them. Kids love them, and they're almost greaseless."

Kelly caught his sleeve and tugged him over to where one of the workers was setting out trays of white rolls at the serving window. "Here's another thing I'd change," she told him. "Whole-wheat rolls would give the kids more vitamins and fiber. And see the butter?" She nodded at the yellow pats resting on their tiny paper trays just beyond the rolls. "That's more fat that the kids don't need. If she must serve rolls, she should serve them with honey or jam. Sugar isn't so good for their teeth, but it's healthier than butter by far."

"And if you were to do it the way you liked?" David asked. Looking down, he touched a fingertip to her hand, which still grasped his sleeve.

With a start, she let him go, her hand tingling as if she'd bumped a red-hot oven rack. "Ideally?" she said, her mind very far from food for an instant. She brought it back with an effort. "Ideally, I'd serve them a slice of homemade Boston brown bread, or a slice of zucchini or pumpkin bread, with a dollop of yogurt cheese as a spread. Maybe sweeten the yogurt cheese with a dash of honey or apple sauce."

She moved away, pretending to be interested in the cake, which the blond worker was slicing into squares. "Here's more fat," she said over her shoulder. "I don't know the recipe for this, but I imagine it's full of eggs, whole milk, bleached flour, and most likely lard was used in both the batter and the icing. Am I right?" she asked the woman.

The blond looked up at her with timid, washed-out blue eyes. "Bertie says I'm not supposed to talk to you," she muttered, glancing around for the chief cook, who was staring cold daggers at them from her position at the head of the serving counter.

"Oh, for Pete's sake!" David growled. "If she gives you any trouble, Mrs. Cottrell, you just come to me."

"You won't be here next Monday when she passes out the week's assignments," Mrs. Cottrell retorted with surprising spirit. "I'll be on dishwashing for the rest of the year!"

"Just nod if there's lard in the recipe," Kelly suggested.

Mrs. Cottrell pursed her lips and nodded, then ducked her head as Bertie Higgins called, "Laura, what's keeping you? Our kids are here."

Kelly turned to see the first classes being shepherded into the cafeteria by their teachers. She touched David's arm. "Let's go watch from outside, shall we?" Without looking to see if he followed, she led the way out into the cafeteria. But from the prickling sensation between her shoulder blades, she was certain he was close behind.

Kelly stopped by the cooler where the milk was stored. As each child filed past, he chose a carton and set it on his tray. "They have a choice of whole, skim or chocolate whole milk," she noted as David joined her. "But no one over two years old should drink whole milk. So I'd limit the choice to skim and low-fat milk. And I'd see if I could find a dairy who'd supply chocolate skim milk, since that seems most popular."

They made a slow circuit of the room. "Mrs. Higgins was right—they don't eat their beans," she murmured, again leaning close to David's ear so that he'd hear her above the bedlam. "I don't blame them. If you cook out all their texture and vitamins, beans are pretty awful. I'd steam them for a few minutes—without butter—then offer them in a cold bean or rice salad with a dash of vinaigrette."

She looked down as a small girl stopped at her feet. "It's the Chicken Lady!" the child announced to the world at large. "Told you! See her hair?"

"Hi!" Kelly said, feeling her cheeks start to burn. Beside her, David chuckled.

"Did you bring us more cookies?" the child demanded.

"Not today." But it was obvious the child had liked them, and Kelly shot David a triumphant look.

Someone tapped her hand, and she looked down at a freckle-faced boy she remembered from her last visit. "Are you Suki's mom?" he asked with a hint of a lisp.

"Yes, honey. You know Suki?"

He nodded enthusiastically. "Everybody knows Suki! She's neat! She gave me a stick of gum at recess yesterday." He fished a crumpled, paper-wrapped wad from his pants pocket. "I kept it," he confided in a hoarse whisper.

If Kelly had had any gum, she'd have awarded him the whole pack for this revelation. She beamed as he darted away.

David chortled. "Watch out for that kid," he said, his breath caressing her ear. "Another eight years, and you'll be tripping over him every time you open your front door. Him and every other boy in town."

"You think so?" she asked eagerly. It was one thing to believe your daughter walked on water. But it was even nicer to hear it from a total stranger. Not that David was that anymore, she realized as their eyes met. Quickly she looked away as she felt her breath quicken. Darn him, what was it about the man that made her feel so... so vulnerable?

"I know it, Chicken Lady," David assured her. "Suki's as much of a knockout as her mom."

She didn't know how to handle a compliment coming from David. Kelly looked away, then jumped as he took her arm.

"Seen enough?" he asked, and when she nodded, her eyes apparently absorbed by a crayon mural taped to the far wall, he added, "Good. Because talking about food has made me hungry. Can I buy you lunch?"

No, a small inner voice answered instantly. That wouldn't be wise. "I'm... rather busy," she hedged, scrambling to construct an excuse. Jane had agreed to work a split shift today at Pure and Simple, so Kelly had plenty of time before she had to relieve her employee. But she had no desire to spend that time with David Whittaker.

"But you've got to eat," he countered. "And we'll make it a short lunch if you like."

She didn't like. Her stomach felt as if it enclosed a whole flock of starlings exploding into flight. "I tell you what!" she blurted. "Why don't we eat here? Then you'll see what I mean about a greasy meal."

David winced. "Wasn't exactly what I had in mind."

"But if the kids have to take it, then maybe you should," she teased, deliberately putting him on the defensive.

His brows twitched. "Okay. Let me have a word with Mrs. Higgins."

Her hands creeping to their opposite elbows in a nervous hug, she let out a shaky breath. Good, she'd handled that well. How hard could it be, sitting across from David at one of these tables, with a chorus of childish comments making it difficult to hear each other and impossible to talk? She could handle that for twenty minutes or so.

She looked up as a bell rang. The children scrambled to empty and stack their lunch trays, then assemble in lines near the door as their teachers returned to collect them. A few minutes later, she spotted Mr. Peabody marching a covey of children into the room. Suki's fair head gleamed at the tail end of the straggling line. Engaged in vivacious conversation with the girl at her side, she hadn't yet noticed her mother.

Kelly drew a deep breath and headed for the teacher. Here was another person to whom she owed amends. "Mr. Peabody?"

By the time she'd paid her regards and apologized for her previous overzealousness, Suki had spotted her. Not knowing if her daughter would care to be owned in public, Kelly gave her a broad wink. But to her delight, Suki hurried to her side. "Mommy, what are you doing here?"

"Tell you later, hon-bun." Kelly touched her cheek.

Suki's violet eyes swept over her mother's suit. "You look pretty," she decided judiciously.

It was ridiculous how much the approval of one's own child mattered, but it did. Kelly wanted to hug her, but she knew how Suki would take that in public. "Thank you, Sukums. How's your day going?"

Suki beamed. "I won the spelling bee, and Carol Anne invited me to her birthday party!"

"That's wonderful, honey." She watched with pride as Suki skipped off to a table to join five other little girls.

"Okay," David said, catching her arm. "Lunch is served."

"We're eating in here?" she asked as he drew her through the kitchen doorway. It would be hard enough eating under David's teasing eyes. If she had to try to stomach Mrs. Higgins's cooking while that formidable woman glared at her, she was guaranteed a major case of heartburn.

"Not exactly." On the counter by the rear entrance to the kitchen sat a cardboard box. David collected it, then held open the screen door for her. "I persuaded Bertie to pack a picnic lunch for us. All this noise is giving me a headache."

And the idea of a picnic alone with David Whittaker gave Kelly an instant case of the cold, fluttering shim-shams, as her mother used to call an attack of nerves. She shot him a horrified glance.

But it was too late. Catching her arm, he eased her out the back door and into the delicious warmth of a sunny spring day. "Let me show you where we used to play hooky," he said lightly. His hand sliding down her arm until his fingers meshed with hers, he drew her across the back parking lot and onto a trail that parted the woods beyond.

CHAPTER EIGHT

SUNLIGHT FILTERED through branches covered with swelling buds, and somewhere a song bird called. Underfoot, the trail was damp and patterned with children's footprints. Kelly stumbled as one of her heels sank into the sand. "Sorry," David said, slowing down. He transferred his grip from her hand to her arm.

Far off, she could hear two sentinel crows crying their intruder call. Nearby, she could hear David's soft breathing and the subterranean thump of her heart. That was all. "Is it much farther?" she asked. The silence seemed to press in on her with heavy, stroking hands.

"Not far at all," he answered. "That was always its one disadvantage. We used to skip out at recess. But if a teacher noticed we were gone, she'd send the principal after us. I was marched back up this trail with a hand on my collar more times than I care to recall." He grinned and glanced around. "Trees don't seem quite as tall as I remember. This used to be the forest primeval."

It still was to Kelly. Around her the spirits of the trees felt like restless dreamers, stirring and stretching in the sun's returning warmth. A few more days and they'd awaken. Here spring would be an explosion of unfurling, translucent green, a leafy shout of exultation.

"Look." David caught a branch and pulled it toward her.

"Pussy willows!" Kelly laughed with delight and touched a silver bud. "It's been a long winter." She felt like one of the trees, a sleeper ready to shrug off the icy nightmares of winter and waken to tender warmth.

"Yes." David's fingers tightened on her arm.

"Oh!" Kelly cried as they rounded a bend. Several yards wide and perhaps a foot deep, a stream rippled across their path, spreading to make a sun-flecked pool, then narrowing as it twisted back into the undergrowth. "No wonder you came here!" Beyond the stream, a grassy bank was crowned by a granite boulder. Its sunlit ledges provided a series of perches that would have delighted a gang of small boys.

"We called it the hooky brook. Hmm, looks like a stepping stone or two is missing," David said, surveying the rocks that formed a haphazard path across the pool. "Or they've rearranged them to keep the girls out."

"Ha!" Kelly reclaimed her hand. "It takes more than that to keep us out nowadays." Standing on tiptoe so that her heels wouldn't touch the mossy stones, she spread her arms and started across. "Always did, in fact."

"Mmm," David agreed behind her. "Funny how that doesn't bother me anymore. Seemed a terrible nuisance at eight."

The smile in his voice brought an answering one to her face. Then a stone rolled underfoot. Kelly let out a squeak as she wobbled.

"Easy!" From behind, David caught her shoulder, his fingers pressing into the softness above her collarbone as he steadied her.

"Whew!" Kelly stood very still. "Thanks." Below the glittering, sliding water, the sandy bottom of the pool reflected the sun. She stood surrounded by liquid gold, with a sound echoing in her ears, as if David's fingers had plucked a single gold wire stretched taut within her.

"I should have offered to carry you," David said, his voice huskier as his fingertips stirred against her skin.

The thought of being lifted in his arms sent her heart into her throat like a pheasant being flushed from cover. She shook her head, then flinched as her chin grazed his knuckles. Catching his fingers, she lifted them from her shoulder, then dropped them as she negotiated the last few stones. "No need," she said, stepping onto the bank.

"So I see." He landed nimbly beside her. "Grass or stone?" he added, laughter and something else threading through the question.

The smooth slope of grass looked too...soft, without boundaries. "Stone," she said primly. But that was a mistake, she realized as she reached the base of the car-size boulder. In a straight skirt and heels, the first toehold was a good foot higher than she could hope to manage.

"It'll be dry and warm," David agreed. His hands closing around her waist, he turned her back to face him.

"On second thought..." she gasped. Too late—his grip tightened, his fingers imprinting themselves on her body as he lifted her. He set her on a ledge some four feet above the ground. She found that she'd caught his forearms for balance and that she now held them tightly.

Beneath the sleeves of his jacket, his arms felt rock hard and so much brawnier than her own that it was vaguely shocking. As if he and she were two different species, constructed from different molds.

His eyes had gone very dark as his pupils expanded. Her skirt had ridden up, baring her knees. As Kelly pressed them together, her nylons made a tiny rasping sound that seemed outrageous in the silence. Slowly they released each other. "If you'd told me twenty-five years ago that there'd come a day when I'd help a girl up the Fort Rock...!" David said, laughing under his breath.

He'd left their lunch on the far bank while he shepherded her across. As he picked his way back to the box, Kelly drew a steadying breath. David had done nothing, really, to make her feel what she was feeling. Perhaps it wasn't him at all. Just that it was the first day of spring and no man had touched her for so long. Leaning back against the warm stone, she folded her legs up beside her and smoothed her skirt.

"Whew, I'm starving!" David said as he set the box on the ledge, then hoisted himself easily alongside her. "All this thinking about food..." He unpacked two plates covered with foil and handed her one, then utensils to go with it.

It was safer to look at the food than him, though she wasn't hungry. The sight of three pieces of greasy chicken, a heap of sodden beans and cold gravy congealing on a lump of instant mashed potatoes did nothing to whet her appetite. Selecting the roll as the least of all evils, she ate it without butter. It was good, she had to admit. Its crust had been brushed with more butter, and its texture was light and airy. Bertie Higgins could cook, even if she was doing herself no favors by her choice of recipes.

"You haven't tried the chicken," David observed as he put down a well-gnawed drumstick.

"No." Kelly was surprised to see he'd finished his potatoes already. He had the appetite of the small boy who'd first climbed this rock, and a child's unblinking wonder. His eyes traced the flight of a blue jay across the clearing, fixed on a jet overhead, then swung back to her, all with that same zestful intensity. Putting down his plate, he took the drumstick off Kelly's. *Good, let him have it,* she thought.

But David had other plans. He held the drumstick to her lips. "Eat," he commanded. "It's no fair judging someone's food if you haven't tried it."

"David, I can tell what it's like just by looking."

"Not good enough, Ms. Bouchard." He touched the drumstick to her bottom lip. "I won't take your suggestions seriously if you don't put your mouth where your money is."

With her back against the rock, she couldn't retreat. And if she turned her head aside, she'd likely get the drumstick smeared across a cheek. With a sigh of exaggerated patience, she took a grudging nibble while he held the piece. "Satisfied?" she growled once she'd swallowed.

"Uh-uh." He brought the drumstick back to her lips. "Eat it all."

She glared at him, but his smile only widened. She shrugged and reached to take it from him. But he wouldn't let go. Kelly found her hand closing over his fingers instead of the chicken. They lifted the piece together and hastily she bit off a chunk, then as quickly released him. Trying to erase the tactile memory of warm, resilient flesh, she flattened her hand against the ledge and rubbed the gritty stone.

"That's better," David applauded, his voice rougher than before. "Tastes good, doesn't it?"

She shrugged and was suddenly conscious of her breasts as she did so. "Grease tastes good. That doesn't mean it's good for you." She took another bite as he held the piece up. She found herself inhaling deeply, trying to distinguish the odor of his skin from that of warm chicken.

"It is sort of greasy," David admitted while she swallowed that bite. Delicately, slowly, he wiped his thumb across her moistened lips. "And I'm afraid they forgot to pack the napkins. Bless 'em." With just his fingertip, he outlined the shape of her lips.

His finger didn't feel steady. So it wasn't just her. He was feeling this, too. "Don't!" she said breathlessly, turning her head aside.

"No?" His hand dropped away. "Why not?"

"Because..." She couldn't think of a coherent reason, not with him leaning as close as he was. The rhythm of her breathing had gone all wrong. One second it came too fast, the next she forgot to inhale.

Her hand was splayed against the rock. She flinched as he stroked a fingertip across it. "How... long have you been divorced?" he asked.

She bit her lip. "Six months, and I don't want to talk about it."

"Okay," he agreed without resentment. Light as an exploring ant, his fingertip outlined her hand. "What *do* you want to talk about?"

She didn't want to talk. She wanted to scramble down off this rock and run for her life.

"You wanted to talk about food the first time I met you," he reminded her, a note of teasing creeping into his voice. "Why are you so... fixed on the subject, Kelly? Your mother was a flower child and you were raised on a strict diet of granola and bean sprouts?"

"Hardly." She found herself telling him about Helen, their years of cooking together at the clam shack, then somehow, astonishingly, since it was a topic she never mentioned to anyone, her years of being a shy, chubby teenager.

"I see." He brushed the back of his knuckles down her sleeve. "It's hard, not being accepted at that age. I had a taste of that myself, my last couple of years in high school."

Was he referring to the scandal over his father and his zoning tricks? She turned to study him, but he didn't elaborate. Instead, his hand rose to her face and she felt her hair stir. It was starting to escape its pins. He brushed the flyaway curls again and the sensation feathered out across her scalp. She felt as if he'd stroked her with a piece of sun-warmed, crumpled silk. That her skin itself had turned to silk.

"You're looking more like yourself," he teased. "When you walked in the door this morning, I hardly recognized you."

He didn't think she could be practical? Businesslike? Was that what he meant? Just because she sold kelp and ginseng instead of typewriter ribbons or real estate, it didn't make her any less competent. She was tired of being considered a wild-eyed, fuzz-brained fanatic just because she had the nutritional sense to prefer brown rice to white. "It's getting late," she said, though she had no idea what time it was. "I'm due at my shop." She swung her legs down from the ledge to dangle them, sending one of her pumps flying. "Darn!"

"I'll get it." David let himself down from the ledge, but instead of fetching her shoe, he busied himself gathering their picnic debris.

She had half a mind to jump down and fetch it herself, but if she did, she'd ruin her hose. It wouldn't be fun, walking back with grit in her shoe so she sat there, kicking her heels and looking down on David's thick, glossy hair. His downswept lashes were incredibly long for a man. She could imagine the tiny, feathery sensation if she were to brush a fingertip across them. Her face warmed as she realized what she was thinking.

He put the last plate in the box, then turned and found her shoe.

"Thanks." She held out her hand for it, but he ignored the gesture. Instead, he gripped her ankle. His fingers were incredibly warm. They curled right around her bones, encircling her like a living manacle, then squeezed gently. The sensation shot up her leg like a comet raking across the sky trailing a tail of white fire.

"You've legs like a colt," he murmured. Lifting her foot, he ran one fingertip up its sole. He looked up, his eyes searching, as she shivered.

"Could I have my shoe, please?" Her face must have been fiery red. She felt as if she were melting, her skin fusing with his.

"Certainly." He slid it neatly onto her foot.

"Now if you'll stand back..." She would hop down from this ledge and wouldn't stop moving till she'd reached civilization.

"Here's a better idea." David slid one arm under her knees, the other around her back. As she let out a squeak of protest, he lifted her.

"David, put me down!" she yelped, kicking her legs.

"Sure, in a minute." He moved purposefully down the bank.

"No—I mean now!" But he'd already stepped out onto the first stone, and there was nothing but water beneath her waving feet.

David stopped. "Now?" he challenged, starting to grin.

Blast the man! She glared up at him, trying to contain her outrage. But intruding on that emotion was the soft, insistent thud of a heartbeat where her breast rested against his chest.

"Well?" His taunt was barely louder than a whisper.

"Rat!" she muttered. She'd hooked one arm around his neck, but the treacherous fingers of that hand might have belonged to someone else. In spite of her indignation, they itched to explore his hair, the texture of the jacket that curved across his broad shoulders, the lobe of his ear. She clenched her hand till her nails bit into her palm.

"Here I'm playing Sir Walter Raleigh and you call me a rat? Maybe I *should* put you down." He started to lower her, then paused as her reflexes took hold and she clutched him tight. "No?" he taunted.

"No," she agreed, her voice icy. Now they were molded together. She could feel his heart beating beneath her own. He felt as if he were idling, like a big engine in neutral. She tried to loosen her grip on his shoulders, but she was too tense to relax.

"Good," he said so softly that she felt the word vibrating in his chest more than heard it.

There was no sensation of effort in the way he carried her. She seemed to float above golden water, the shudder of their hearts counterpointing the rippling stream below. It would have been so easy to surrender to his easy strength, but the last time she'd surrendered her heart...

Panic blossomed within her like a dark flower. Sinking her teeth into her lip, Kelly willed herself not to struggle. He'd free her more quickly if she simply waited until they reached dry land. But it was so hard! So hard, when one part of her longed to turn her head and press her face into the side of his neck, to simply close her eyes and inhale his warm essence.

Then they were climbing the bank. She drew a shivering breath as David stooped to set her on her feet. "Thanks," she murmured as if he was a stranger who'd held a door for her. She started up the path.

"Kelly," he called. "Kelly!" he repeated, catching up to her. His hand slid from her arm to her wrist, then his fingers meshed with her own.

His bones were slightly too wide for hers. As they spread her fingers to press against the sensitive valleys between, the sensation was stunningly intimate, his body imposing its shape upon hers. She turned to look at him. "David, you've got to understand. I'm not looking for somebody to carry me across streams. I'm not looking for somebody to hold hands with." She tried a pleading smile. "I'm not *looking*, don't you see?"

"Okay..." he said slowly, dropping her hand. "I can understand that." He drew a deep breath. "But have you ever noticed that it's when you're *not* looking that you seem to stumble over the nicest things? You don't go looking for rainbows on wet days—they sneak up on you. You turn around and—wham!—there it is."

"Maybe," she said, unconvinced. "But..." She shook her head. *No.* Fighting the urge to break into a run, she started walking. "I'll write up my suggestions for Mrs. Higgins," she said, retreating from the uncertainty he represented to the one thing in life she was sure of. "But I'm afraid it won't do any good."

He let out a hiss of impatience—this wasn't what he wanted to talk about. But when she kept walking, her face averted, he asked, "Why not?"

"Who's going to make her put them into practice, David? You? Mrs. Cottrell was right. You can't save her from dishwashing detail if Mrs. Higgins wants to bully her. And you certainly can't make Bertie Higgins use skim milk in her mashed potatoes if she wants to use whole, or make sure she's broiling if she wants to deep-fry. She's queen of that kitchen and she's going to do it her way the second you take your eyes off her."

"I suppose you're right," David conceded.

"We're back where we started," she insisted, flinching as his shoulder brushed hers. "Those menus need changing from the ground up, and it's going to take outside help to do it. You need to hire a dietitian. What if you hired one as a consultant, just till the end of the school year? She could give Mrs. Higgins a whole set of new recipes to follow that would be harder for her to sabotage."

They'd reached the final bend beyond which the school would be in view. David caught her wrist and swung her to face him. "We can't do it," he said, his eyes scanning her face. "How many times do I have to tell you? We don't have the money. And I think it would alienate most of the voters, just when we need their approval the most. This is no time to be wasting their tax money on ditsy proposals."

"This isn't a ditsy proposal and it's not a waste of money!" she flared. "Mrs. Higgins is feeding the kids food that's bad for them. That's a pure and simple fact!" She tried to jerk away, but he held on, his face hardening.

"The voters aren't going to agree with you, Kelly. Most of them grew up on Mrs. Higgins's cooking and they seem healthy enough. I don't agree with you myself, though you have a point or two. But the food tastes good. That chicken was great." He took a slow breath, as if he was trying to back away from the steady escalation of tension between them. "Look," he said, his thumb stroking the side of her wrist. "Aren't you blowing this out of proportion?"

Was she? But with his caress crisping her nerves from wrist to spine, no more reasoned thought was possible. She was lashing out on instinct, creating as much space between herself and David as she could—that was what mattered. She needed room to breathe, to be Kelly. She'd only just started finding herself, finding her way in the world. She didn't need this man with his gentle hands and his piercing eyes pushing her off course. "No, I'm not!" she blazed, yanking her hand free. "But since you're not going to take this seriously, David, I guess I'll have to take another tack."

His eyes narrowed. "Meaning?"

"Meaning that Elliot Freeling called for an interview yesterday and I put him off, since I thought you really meant to help me. But since you don't, I guess it's time to talk to him. Now that I've seen Mrs. Higgins's kitchen I can give him some specific facts. If he wants to do an article or two, I think we can really stir up the town."

"I didn't arrange this tour so you could use your observations against us," he pointed out.

"No, you arranged this tour to pacify me, didn't you? It kept me away from Freeling, and you hoped that I'd feel what I was doing was useful, even though my suggestions couldn't change a single thing."

"Is that what you think?" he asked bitterly.

Did she believe he was that cynical? He was certainly smart enough to manipulate her like a puppet, but would he? She bit her lip.

"Fine," David said when she didn't answer. "Then we know where we stand, don't we? Go talk with Freeling and be damned. It won't do you a bit of good." He stalked off toward the school.

She stared after his broad shoulders, the panic seeping out of her like air from a punctured balloon. "Fine," she whispered.

She drew a deep, shaky breath and felt it swirl around the emptiness within. "Fine. I'll do that." Yet somehow the decision made her feel anything but fine.

CHAPTER NINE

VICTORIA COCKED HER HEAD, her peacock-feather earring brushing her narrow shoulder, and studied Kelly's face. "What about that theory of yours you once told me? That if you're blue, then that's when you should paste on a big smile." She frowned, trying to remember the rest of it. "'Cause when you smile, your brain feels the smile muscles working, and it thinks you must be happy. So—voilà!—you start being happy."

Kelly tried a weak smile, but her brain wasn't fooled. She sighed and stared around her empty shop. It was Friday, and Victoria had just pried the story of yesterday's disastrous picnic out of her.

Victoria turned a small, aimless circle on her red spike heels. "But I still don't see why you're so down. Just because David Whittaker carried you across the hooky brook. He could carry me to the town dump—I wouldn't complain."

"I don't know." Kelly sighed, slouching down farther over the counter. "It's just..." That she'd driven him away? He'd not be back after yesterday's rejection. She shook her head. Why should that make her sad? She didn't need him. Didn't want him. Wasn't even sure she liked him.

No, that's not true, an inner voice objected. She liked him. A lot.

But do you trust him? her devil's advocate inquired slyly.

Maybe that was the problem. She'd once liked Larry, but trusting him had been a dreadful mistake. Somehow David felt like an even larger disaster looking for a chance to happen to her. She didn't want to care for the wrong man ever again.

"I guess you're just not ready yet," Victoria decided.

That was as good a way as any to sum it up, Kelly decided. And she was tired of talking about it. "Won't be ready for years," she agreed.

"But that doesn't mean you can't have fun," Victoria protested. "I mean, who says you have to get serious? Play him along for laughs if he wants to play. You might as well use him, since he's trying to use you."

"What do you mean?" Kelly asked, then regretted it.

"Well..." Victoria looked uncomfortable, as if she also wished she hadn't started this line of thought. "It doesn't...occur to you that making a play for you is one way to get you off his back? If you start dating Whittaker, are you going to keep speaking out about cafeteria food?" She caught her single snowy lock of hair and frowned at it. "That way, he could get on with his plans to win approval for the new school—and he enjoys you as a bonus."

Could that have been David's purpose? Kelly's stomach twisted at the thought. But the alternative to Victoria's theory was almost as hard to swallow. As heart-stoppingly sexy as David was, surely he could find someone more glamorous than a frizzy-haired freckle farm like her. Someone sensible, since he didn't like feckless, unconventional types. "I dunno," she mumbled. She didn't know anything. That was probably why she was so blue. Confusion wasn't comfortable.

A tall, thin figure strode into the shop. Elliot Freeling fumbled in his jacket pocket while his eyes swung slowly around the room.

He reminded Kelly of a great blue heron—sharp of beak and dour of eye, with that rather glum, deliberate air of the big wading bird. His washed-out blue eyes fixed on Victoria, blinked, then sliced past her to skewer Kelly. "Ms. Bouchard." He dragged a notebook out of his pocket and flipped it open in a single motion. "It was good of you to call me."

She'd done so the day before on reaching the store. Now, when it was too late to back out, she was wondering if it had been a good idea.

"Catch you later," Victoria called, departing. As she passed Freeling, she raised her plucked brows in a mock flirtatious salute, and his head jerked back in a birdlike tic of surprise.

He was almost attractive in a dried-out way, Kelly decided, though it took Victoria to notice it. The editor must be in his early fifties, though somehow he seemed older. "I've never been interviewed before," she said as she brought out a stool from behind the counter, then retreated to her own. "I don't know what to say."

"Just answer the questions, that'll do nicely." Freeling fished in the other sagging pocket of his ancient tweed jacket. Its sleeve was missing a button, Kelly noted, as he pulled out a folded newspaper. "This interview will be a follow-up to the article on your detainment by the police that came out yesterday. And I used you as subject for my lead editorial, as well. But I suppose you've seen this already?"

As she accepted the paper, Kelly had to admit she had not.

Freeling's mouth turned down. "We come out Tuesdays, Thursdays and Saturdays. Have two reporters besides myself—I'm also editor and publisher. You'll want to get a subscription."

"I'll do that," Kelly agreed hastily. "I advertise with you, of course, but..." She drummed her fingertips on the counter. "You know, what I'm wondering is..." She looked up at the newspaperman. "I'm wondering why you're doing this, Mr. Freeling?"

"It's news," he said promptly. "Not every day a parent gets thrown in jail around here for trying to change school policy."

"Oh. I wondered . . . I thought maybe you were . . ."

"Sympathetic to your cause?" Freeling's smile was austere. "Let me be frank with you, Ms. Bouchard. You make an interesting story, but I couldn't care less about kids or what they eat. Far as I'm concerned, kids are just short, mouthy, illiterate people." He pulled out a pen from his shirt pocket and jabbed the button to make its point pop out. "Unfortunately, most of 'em grow up to be tall, mouthy, illiterate people, but that's another story." He flipped to a new page in his notebook. "To my mind, people should be born at forty. That's about the age they start to be interesting, if they ever do."

Whew! And she'd thought Victoria was cynical. Kelly mustered a noncommittal smile. Freeling was going to be her ally? This must be what they meant by politics making strange bedfellows. "I see," she said. "Well . . . what would you like to ask?"

Half an hour later, Freeling nodded his grizzled head in satisfaction. "That should about do it, Ms. Bouchard. Oh, one last question . . ." He looked at her sternly. "Just what do you plan to do next?"

Kelly gulped. Each time she took action, she seemed to get herself in deeper trouble. These past few weeks, she'd felt as if she were picking her way blindfolded across a bog. She sighed softly between her teeth. Oh, well, by now she'd wandered so far onto shaky ground she might as well go forward as try to find her way back. "I haven't delivered the petition yet," she reminded Freeling. "So I guess the next step is to give that to the school committee. They're still working on next year's budget, I understand. And since the public's allowed to speak, I guess that's just what I'll do. I'll tell the committee and anyone else who'll listen about what

I saw in Mrs. Higgins's kitchen—why it's so unhealthy. And I'll pass out my fact sheets to the audience." She nodded at the copies she'd given Freeling.

He nodded. "After my article comes out, you may find more people wanting to sign your petition before you turn it in."

"I'll get there early, then." Kelly stood as the journalist rose. "You've really been a darling about this, Mr. Freeling."

He grimaced. "All in a day's work." He tucked his notebook into his pocket and, with the loss of that prop, suddenly looked less certain of himself. "Well..."

"Thank you." Kelly shook his hand, finding it as dry as old paper. She considered, then rapidly rejected, the notion of giving him a bottle of her favorite herbal moisturizer. He might think she was bribing the press.

That weekend and the early part of the following week, Kelly stayed busier than usual, reordering inventory and rearranging shelves, readying her and Suki's clothes for spring, cooking a month's worth of casseroles and soups and freezing them in double portions. But in spite of all that activity, the days dragged by. *Blame it on the weather,* she told herself Tuesday, when she mailed off her suggestions on how to reform Bertie Higgins's cooking methods to David. It had been gray and drizzly since Sunday.

But Wednesday when the sun came out at last, she was still feeling low at the end of the day. David would have received her letter that morning. Somehow she'd hoped—no, that was the wrong word. Somehow she'd *thought* she'd get some response, even if it was just a furious phone call to tell her that her ideas were impossible, impractical, expensive and utterly impolitic. By eleven she gave up and trudged off to bed. *What did you expect?* her inner critic jeered as she hugged her pillow and buried her nose in its softness. *You get in the man's way, you reject his advances, so why on earth should he call?* And why on earth should she care?

The following night she stood outside the high school, handing out her fact sheets to the incoming crowd. "Hello, could I give you some information about school lunches?" She passed the papers to a couple.

"Well, somebody better give us some information!" the man growled as he grabbed the sheets. He forged on toward the entrance, his wife almost trotting to keep up with him.

What was that about? Kelly stared after him, then shrugged and turned back. "Hi! Could I give you some papers to read?"

"You certainly may," a woman said warmly. "And I bet you're Kelly Bouchard. I read the article in the *Dartmouth Daily.*"

"Nut!" a passing man said succinctly. He put up his hands to ward off Kelly's fact sheets and hurried up the stairs.

"Takes all kinds," the woman observed, shaking her head. "Oh, that's your petition? Yes, I'd love to sign it."

Minutes before the meeting was to start, Kelly packed up her papers. She'd collected perhaps a dozen more signatures. But most of the townspeople were moving too fast to be waylaid. There was an urgency to the crowd that seemed out of proportion to a simple school-committee meeting. Hurrying after the stragglers, Kelly slipped into the auditorium.

A graying, heavyset woman was just bringing the meeting to order, with the explanation that she would be acting chair. "Tonight's program will be a continuation of the line-by-line budget examination, starting with the math department, then on to science. But before that, Mr. Whittaker has a short slide presentation." She gestured vaguely at David, who sat to her left, then at a screen suspended from the ceiling behind the committee's table. "He's brought in the architectural plans for the new high school to give you an idea of what it will look like—once we pass the bond issue to build it. And of course we're all hoping for your support on that matter."

"Yeah, but first we got something more important to talk about!" A man in the middle of the auditorium had risen to his feet. "I want to know what in heck is going on down at Oake Elementary!" He was seconded by a loud rumble from the crowd.

The chairwoman bridled. "I beg your pardon, but did I recognize you?"

"You know darn well who I am, Ellen May, and don't change the subject! What's going on down there? Has Bertie flipped her wig? She served the kids roast turkey last Friday, right?"

Ellen May didn't answer—she was conferring with her neighbor. David frowned and leaned closer to listen.

"So what does she serve them on Monday?" the man continued at a near shout. "She serves them turkey sandwiches—without mayo. Okay, well, maybe that makes sense—we all got to put up with leftovers—"

"But then she serves them turkey hash on Tuesday!" cried a woman in the front row. "And Wednesday it's turkey tetrazzini."

"Right!" the man yelled over the rising mutter of the crowd. "And you know what it was today? Turkey croquettes with turkey soup! My kid's gonna come home *gobbling* if she doesn't cut this out. You guys get a bargain on a truckload of turkey or something? What gives?"

Bertie Higgins was on the warpath, that much was plain. And Kelly could guess why, since the turkey tantrum had apparently started the day after her kitchen tour. She shot David a stricken look and found he was glaring directly at her. She'd made some remark about substituting turkey for fried chicken within Mrs. Higgins's hearing, hadn't she? Apparently the cook meant to ram low-fat turkey down everyone's throat till they screamed for mercy.

Another woman stood and Kelly recognized her as one of her customers. "While we're on the subject of food, I'd like to ask the school committee to address the issues brought up in several *Dartmouth Daily* articles this week. If the school lunches are unhealthy, just how does the committee plan to correct the situation?"

"That's what I'd like to know!" someone else shouted.

The chairwoman tapped the gavel and kept on tapping it until the crowd's comments faded. "One moment please. If everyone would just be patient." The school committee went into a huddle.

It seemed that David was doing most of the talking, while the others either nodded their heads or protested. Finally all heads turned toward the audience. As seven pairs of eyes seemed to focus on her, Kelly scrunched lower in her seat. David was blaming this all on her, wasn't he?

The huddle broke, and the committee members returned to their seats. David pulled his microphone into position. "The committee is aware of the situation at Oake Elementary," he noted calmly.

Kelly caught her bottom lip in her teeth. He was sharp, wasn't he? David had just neatly skirted the fact of *when* the school committee had become aware of the problem.

"It happens that we've been reassessing the lunch program," he continued. "Mrs. Higgins, as Lunch Director, has been experimenting with the menus."

"Yeah, but turkey five days in a row?" yelped the original objector.

"We agree, Mrs. Higgins has been a bit . . . too enthusiastic, and we'll certainly speak to her. In addition to that, we'd like to announce that a townswoman with experience in restaurant management and nutrition has volunteered to act as a menu consultant. She'll be instituting a trial program at Oake Elementary to see if low-fat lunches are acceptable to the students."

He'd done it! After all his resistance to her pleas, David had turned around and found someone, after all. Kelly gave him a radiant smile and a thumbs-up. He wasn't as stiff-necked as she'd—

"Would Ms. Bouchard please stand so that everyone can give her a round of applause?" David asked, his voice much too smooth.

He means me? Kelly's mouth formed an "O." She stared in horror at his dawning smirk. Then, as David pointed her out, the people to either side nudged her to her feet. She grabbed the back of the seat before her and peered around wildly at the sea of cheering faces. He meant her, and by restaurant experience he must mean her mother's clam shack. *I'm supposed to be a consultant to Bertie Higgins? She'll eat me alive!* Kelly's knees went weak and she sat again with a thump.

As the applause died down, David continued speaking. "Of course, we all understand that any changes that may be put into effect this year or next will *in no way* increase the school budget. In fact, Ms. Bouchard thinks she can save us some money."

The crowd beamed at Kelly. That was something of which everyone could approve.

"And we trust you understand that changes won't come overnight," David added. "So we're asking everyone to be patient and to give Ms. Bouchard time to do a proper job. We're asking her to report back to this committee in six weeks with her findings."

Six weeks! She was supposed to reform Bertie Higgins and her entire lunch program in six weeks? It couldn't be done.

"Meanwhile," David continued, "the school committee would like to shelve the issue of food until our consultant reports back to us. We've got next year's budget to complete, and we have a school bond issue that..."

Whatever else he said, Kelly was lost in grudging admiration of David Whittaker. With his quick thinking, he'd preempted everyone's complaints by seeming to be on top of the problem. And he'd earned the committee a healthy respite from the issue by asking her to report back in six weeks.

And on a personal level, David had thrown her complaints back in her teeth. *You think something needs changing?* he'd in effect said to her. *So change it.* And with his public announcement, he'd given her no chance to refuse the position.

But that didn't matter. For, with a feeling like that of a parachutist taking her first jump, Kelly realized she had no intention of refusing David's challenge. She didn't know how she'd reform Bertie Higgins in six short weeks, but she sure meant to try.

CHAPTER TEN

WHEN THE MEETING ENDED, Kelly found herself the center of a small mob of congratulatory parents. The consensus seemed to be that it was about time *somebody* did something. But then, she was preaching to the choir here, she reminded herself. Plenty of people had stalked past her up the aisles with looks of wonder or disgust. Clearly not everybody in West Dartmouth agreed with her views. *Well, I'll just have to change that,* she told herself as she waved goodbye to the last of her supporters.

"Got time for a cup of coffee?" Hands jammed casually in his pockets, David sauntered up the aisle.

The thought of sharing a table with him sent her pulse skyrocketing. *Anger,* she told herself, and knew it wasn't so. Her hands flew to her elbows in a protective hug, and her heart seemed to be playing hopscotch in her chest. Darn the man! She didn't need this vulnerability. Not around a man she didn't trust. "I'm afraid I don't," she said. "I'm trying out a new baby-sitter tonight, and I promised I'd be home by eleven."

"We have to discuss this," he insisted.

"What's there to discuss? You're doing fine as a dictator. You've drafted me for six weeks without a by-your-leave, or an is-that-convenient-for-you, Kelly? Did it ever occur to you that I've a store to run? I don't get enough time with Suki as it is, and now, if I have to come up with new recipes—the time to test them, to research their nutritional value, find bulk sources for ingredients..."

"Do you or don't you want the job?" David demanded.

"I...do," Kelly admitted. Darn him, couldn't he at least let her grouse a bit before accepting?

"Good." The corners of his mouth twitched. "I thought you would."

"And if I hadn't?" He'd certainly stuck out his neck far enough in public. "Wouldn't you have felt foolish if I'd stood up and refused?"

"No, but I'd have lost some respect for you," David said.

Kelly blinked. Respect wasn't something she was used to receiving from men. *From Larry,* she corrected herself. Perhaps because he'd been ten years her senior, he'd always—at least it seemed now that he'd always—treated her with a humorous condescension that had bordered on contempt. The thought of earning David's respect—or that she had it already—was unexpectedly heady.

David caught her arm and turned her. "Old Cassidy will lock us in for the night if we don't get out of here," he said, nodding at the janitor who glowered at them from the exit. "Not that that might not be fun..."

Kelly caught her bottom lip in her teeth as he steered her up the aisle. She'd assumed her rejection of him at the nooky brook would have ended such talk. "So when do I start?" she asked briskly.

"Monday, if you like. I'll lay down the law to Bertie tomorrow."

"She's not going to like it."

"You're telling me!" David agreed. "I tried to foist the job off on Ellen May since she was chairing this week, but she wasn't having any."

Kelly laughed. "Since it was your idea, it serves you right."

His fingers tightened, and his smile went rueful. Kelly's heart, which had settled down while they spoke, turned one last cartwheel. *Darn the man!* She started talking fast and furiously about her plans for the lunch program. All through David's abbreviated display of the new high-school plans, she'd made notes and she'd come up with some good ideas. "If Mrs. Higgins will just cooperate, I'm sure we can find menus that the kids will love," she enthused as they reached her van.

"You think so?" David asked absently, his eyes drifting down to her lips, then back to her eyes.

She should get out of there. But something about his gaze seemed to slow the blood in her veins, leaving her soft and sleepy and a little bit dazed. Waiting. "You don't?" she challenged, trying to break the spell. "Why are you letting me do this, then?"

"To get you out of our hair," David said simply. "Why else? I figure in six weeks you'll have convinced yourself that the kids of West Dartmouth prefer greasy pizza." His hand drifted up to catch a curl that had escaped her chignon. "I figure you'll be tuckered out from your do-gooding and ready to let the whole thing drop by then. I'll be winding up the campaign to build the new school, so then maybe we can all get back to normal."

She wasn't feeling normal at the moment, Lord knew. It was part outrage at his frank cynicism, part something else entirely. She shook her head as her hands spread flat on his chest to hold them apart. She shook her head again, wondering just who had stepped closer, David or... "Don't!" she breathed as his head came down.

He paused, his lips hovering over hers. "Why not?" he murmured. His hands settled gently on her shoulders.

"I..." There were many reasons why not, yet she couldn't think of one with him this close. All she could think was that, if she moved even closer and pressed her body to his, she'd feel his heart pounding to match her own. "I'm afraid..." she said on a rising squeak.

His mouth curved in a slow, sweet smile. "I'd figured out that much." His hands moved restlessly on her shoulders. "I meant to apologize to you about the other day at the brook, and now I'm doing it again, aren't I?"

"You don't need to apologize," Kelly protested. But he needed to let her go. *She* needed it.

"No, I don't think I do," David agreed. "As beautiful as you are, what else should I do but this?" Light as a butterfly, his lips touched hers.

But Kelly was too stupefied by his words even to register the kiss, and he ended it immediately when she didn't respond. As his head came up, his brows slanted in question.

"Beautiful?" Kelly repeated. "Nobody's ever—" She stopped.

"Nobody's ever told you that before?" David demanded. The note of incredulity in his voice was more convincing than any compliment. "What about your damned husb—" He cut that off as if he didn't like the word.

No, Larry's approval had been rare and grudging, and more often than not directed to the dress or shoes or hairstyle his money had purchased than to Kelly herself. But she didn't want to think about that. David found her beautiful? A blush of pure pleasure suffused her skin, and this time when he kissed her, her lips moved against his in a shy, disbelieving smile.

"Well, believe it!" David said roughly. Smoothing her throat with the palm of his hand, he tipped her chin up again.

And sanity returned as suddenly as it had vanished. She was standing in a parking lot, about to let David Whittaker kiss her—this was madness. Twisting in his arms, she jammed a hand into her shoulder bag and yanked out her keys. "Yes, well," she babbled, "that's all very nice, but..." She jabbed the key into the lock, turned it frantically. Behind her, David was quietly...laughing? But this was no laughing matter to Kelly.

"Yes, it is," David said, backing up a step as she wrenched open the door and scrambled into the van. "But where's the fire, Red?"

"Baby-sitter!" she snapped, and slammed her door. He was still standing there, his big hands relaxed in his pockets, a grin on his face that was almost silly, when Kelly roared out of the parking lot.

She didn't stop until she hit her first traffic light. Then, when it changed to green, she didn't notice—she was busy touching her lips—until somebody honked. David thought she was beautiful. This was awful.

BUT BY MONDAY MORNING when Kelly let herself in the rear entrance to the cafeteria, her worries about David had taken a back seat to a more immediate problem—how to peaceably share a kitchen with Bertie Higgins.

Looking like a bad-tempered mushroom, Mrs. Higgins was perched on a high stool near the serving counter. A cup of coffee in her hand, she glanced up from the newspaper she was reading. With a sniff, she looked down again.

"Good morning," Kelly said shyly. Approaching the woman, she waited for some sort of acknowledgment.

The cook scowled at her paper.

"Where is everyone else?" Kelly asked after a very long pause.

Mrs. Higgins didn't look up. "Come in later," she grunted.

"Oh." Probably there was a better way to approach their differences than head-on, but Kelly couldn't think of one. Impulsively she pulled up a stool and sat. "Mrs. Higgins, I wonder if there's any way I can apologize to you for the time I first barged in here? I really was out of line that day. Then I wonder if, after I've apologized, we could just...start over? I mean if we're going to work together..." Her voice trailed away as the older woman deliberately licked a finger, then turned a page.

"I see," Kelly said after the silence had stretched thin. "Well, all the same, I wanted to tell you I'm sorry. And I'm sorry now that I've just been dropped on you out of the blue. I didn't ask for this consulting job—I hope David told you that—and I know how hard it is to share a kitchen with another cook. Everybody has their own way of doing things."

Mrs. Higgins finished her coffee and set the cup down with a smack. "What are you cooking today?" she asked, looking at Kelly at last.

"What am *I*..." Kelly repeated incredulously. One look at the woman's face assured her that this was no joke. "I wasn't planning to cook anything for several days, Mrs. Higgins, except to help you with your usual menus. I have all kinds of questions about what you budget per meal, federal dietary regulations..."

"Mr. Whittaker says you have the last word on everything, missy. In my book that means you're the boss. And the boss gives the orders. So what are we cooking today, Boss?"

Kelly opened her mouth, then closed it again. She had to admire the cook's tactic even as she racked her brains on how to respond. She hadn't a clue as to what ingredients were on hand, how to run half the institutional-size appliances, how to apportion tasks, or even how many meals were needed that day. She'd make a botch of the task—which was exactly what Mrs. Higgins wanted. "I'm sorry, but I'd make a mess of it if I tried," she said frankly. "You're the boss—I'm just here to advise."

"And if I don't like your advice?" Mrs. Higgins dropped all pretense of politeness.

Kelly bit her lip. "You know, it's not really my advice. It comes from doctors and scientists, and the research they've been doing these past ten years or so." A giant refrigerator stood against the nearest wall. Kelly crossed to it, opened its door and found what she'd hoped to find. She returned to Mrs. Higgins with a box of butter and slid a quarter-pound stick from the package. "Do you know how much fat the average American eats in a day?" she asked, patting the cold stick against her palm.

Mrs. Higgins shrugged, but the first sign of interest sparked in her blue eyes.

"About this much," Kelly said softly, laying the stick before her. "My mother had a heart attack at forty from eating like that." She looked quickly away from the cook's startled face, and her gaze settled on the coffee urn. "You know, I'm dying for a cup of coffee," she said. "May I?"

"Cups are above the sink," the woman growled.

After that, Kelly made herself small for the rest of the morning. She didn't know if Mrs. Higgins still expected her to take charge of the cooking, but if so, she was in for a disappointment. Kelly was determined to wait her out, even if it meant, come eleven-thirty, they faced a cafeteria full of hungry children with no meal prepared. But she prayed it wouldn't come to that.

While the clock crawled from eight-thirty till nine, then on to ten, Kelly studied the month's menus posted on the wall. She'd come to the conclusion that, where possible, she'd keep the menus the same, but substitute healthier ingredients. That would make the least change for the kids. She knew well enough that children were natural conservatives and picky to boot. But if she substituted tofu for ground meat and part of the cheese in the lasagna recipe, served fish with an oven-baked crust of wheat germ in place of the fried fish sticks... Oh, there were lots of improvements she could make if Mrs. Higgins would just give her the chance.

But though it had seemed for a moment that she had reached the woman, Kelly must have been mistaken. When the rest of the kitchen workers arrived at ten, their fragile truce was over. Mrs. Higgins marched out of her pantry office, where she'd been doing paperwork, and put her troops in motion. Laura Cottrell was to be "salads" for the week, she decreed, and the other two helpers were "baker" and "veggies" respectively.

Apparently Mrs. Higgins was "meats," because she bustled off to a refrigerator to pull out boxes of frozen hamburger patties. Kelly gritted her teeth and tapped the cook's shoulder. "What am I this week?"

"In the way."

"Mrs. Higgins, I'm *here*. You may as well use me."

"Fine!" The cook yanked a tray from a shelf and threw down a pair of gloves. From the pantry she fetched a two-gallon jar of honey and a box in which tiny white paper cups were stacked. "Fill three hundred of these."

I asked for this? Within five minutes, Kelly didn't know if she wanted to laugh or to weep. Honey dripped from her wrists and made golden splashes on the counter and the serving tray. The tiny cups stuck to her gooey fingers, each other, the lip of the honey jar. "Don't you have a funnel?" she gasped, as yet another cup overflowed onto the counter.

"Oh, I forgot to give you one?" Mrs. Higgins asked with saccharine self-reproach. "Try this." She dropped a funnel on the counter and marched off.

But the mouth of the funnel was so tiny the honey could barely drool through it. Kelly stopped after twenty minutes to survey her dismal results. Two hundred and seventy to go. Glancing around for Mrs. Higgins, Kelly instead met Laura Cottrell's gaze. With a furtive glance over her shoulder, the worker pointed her chef's knife at a spot near Kelly's knees.

Beneath the counter stood a stack of clean funnels, one of which had a wide neck and the label "Honey." With a gasp of relief, Kelly seized it. The next time Mrs. Higgins looked the other way, she blew Laura a kiss.

The task went much faster after that, but Kelly might have been wiser to dawdle. When she'd done, Mrs. Higgins put her on onions for tomorrow's American chop suey—some thirty pounds of onions. With tears dripping from her chin, Kelly sliced and diced until the kids arrived.

Still, it was worth it, she told herself stubbornly as she watched the children accept their greasy hamburgers, french fries, corn and cupcakes with trusting pleasure. She could substitute oven-baked potato sticks for the French fries, that would be no problem. But for the burger? Perhaps a skinless cutlet of barbecued turkey. Or perhaps a Sloppy Joe filling, made with tofu instead of the usual ground beef.

Someone tapped her on the back. "You can start cleaning the steam kettle," Mrs. Higgins informed her with a smirk.

Kelly glanced from the waist-high, greasy kettle to the cook, then back again, suppressed a heartfelt sigh, and smiled. "Glad to."

Things went the same way, if not worse, the following day. Clearly Mrs. Higgins had stayed up half the night devising tasks to exhaust Kelly or drive her nuts. Just as clearly, the other kitchen workers sympathized with her plight, but they hardly dared speak to her even when Mrs. Higgins left the room. So Kelly scrubbed five-gallon pots, chopped mountains of onions, cleaned out ovens encrusted with months of baked-on grease, all in dogged silence, her cheery smile waning by the hour. She'd volunteered for this? No! Come to think of it, she had not—David Whittaker had gotten her into this fix. And where was he now, when she was up to her elbows in grease and slimy soapsuds? He'd been the invisible man since Friday.

And it wasn't until Wednesday that he reappeared. Kelly looked up from wringing out her mop to find him lounging against a counter, a frown drawing his dark brows together. "What do you think you're doing?" he demanded.

Kelly blew a wisp of hair out of her eyes and glared back. "What does it look like?" Swabbing the mop along the counter kickboard, she flicked it over the toes of his sneakers.

He took a step back. "You're supposed to be consulting on menus, Kelly, not doing scut work."

"Oh? Tell that to Bertie," Kelly muttered, turning to survey the room. The tile floor gleamed in every direction. She was done.

"I will," David promised. "Where the heck is she?"

"Went home like everybody else." Kelly propped the mop and herself against the counter. She was too tired to contemplate emptying the bucket of dirty water. "Where have you been?" she asked, startling herself as the words popped out. It was none of her business, after all.

"California," David said absently. "A birthday party..."

A wave of resentment swept over her. Here she'd been playing galley slave all week, and he'd been jaunting cross-country to attend a party? And for whom? For no reason she could have explained, she knew instinctively that the birthday celebrant must have been female. "Great! Hope you had a swell time." Spinning away from him, she started across the room to the sink—and tripped over her pail.

With a yelp, she watched the damp floor rise up to meet her. As her feet knocked over the bucket, a wave of dirty water slooshed over her. "Ohhh..." Every vile word known to woman hovered on her lips as she pushed her face and shoulders off the tiles. "Rats," she said inadequately, staring at her ruined floor—then burst into tears.

"Kelly!" David's hands caught her waist and shoulder. "Are you—"

"Oh, I'm fine," she said bitterly, rolling over and propping herself on one elbow. She looked down to find the front of her T-shirt soaked. "Just hunky-dory! Having the time of my life."

"Yeah, I can see that," David said, his voice shimmering with laughter. Grasping her arms, he helped her to a sitting position.

Which meant that now her bottom was wet to match the front, she realized as she felt the water begin to seep through. She swiped at her eyes, tried a rueful smile and couldn't pull it off.

"Sure you didn't hurt yourself?" David's hand curved to fit her cheek. His other hand came up to mirror the first and frame her face between warm, pleasantly rough fingers. His thumbs fanned her cheeks in soothing, repeated caresses, smoothing away tears and wisps of wet hair.

"Yeah," she said shakily. She should tell him to stop that, but it felt so...good.

"Good," he murmured. Leaning forward, he kissed the tip of her nose. When she smiled, he kissed her lips.

A flower of fire unfurled flame red petals, one by one, within her stomach. The sensation was frightening in its intensity. She stiffened her spine and pulled away from him.

His smile sharpened to a searching look, but he let her go without question. "Well..." He looked around aimlessly at the spreading puddle, then back to Kelly, and his lips quivered. "You know what?" he said softly. "You've sure got my vote for the wet T-shirt contest!"

Face pink, she shrugged, then realized that was a mistake as he sucked in his breath. "Well..." She scrambled to her feet. Collecting the fallen mop, she dabbed listlessly at the puddle.

David took the mop and set it aside. "That's the custodian's job, Kelly. He mops every day after school. Bertie didn't tell you?" When she shook her head, he let out a snort. "I'm going to have a word with her. She's been making it hard for you, hasn't she? You're limp as a dishrag."

"Thanks," Kelly said, too tired to resent the comparison. "But no thanks on speaking to Bertie. You'd only make things worse." Stretching her aching back, she glanced at the clock, then started for the back door.

"I'm not going to stand by and let her run you into the ground," David protested at her heels. "That wasn't the idea at all."

"Oh, wasn't it?" Kelly yanked her jacket off the hook by the door and stepped out into a cool spring wind, welcome after the kitchen's muggy heat. "I seem to recall you hoping that I'd be tuckered out in six weeks."

"Did I? Okay, maybe I did, but—"

"But that doesn't mean this job's any less important, just because she's making it hard, David Whittaker." She spun to face him, but kept backing toward her van. "And don't you go making it even harder for me by fussing at Bertie. I'll handle this my own way." She jumped as she bumped against the side of her van. Wearily she fumbled for her keys.

David took them from her and opened the van's door, then handed them back once she'd climbed inside. "Okay," he said quietly, "if that's the way you want it. But if you change your mind, I'm here."

I'm here. The words warmed her from her head to her toes.

His hand closed over her fingers on the steering wheel and squeezed gently. "Now go home and take a bubble bath, then have a nap," he advised.

With a wry laugh, she shook her head. "David, I have a shop to run, remember? I have to relieve my assistant now." Luckily she'd brought a change of clothes with her. "I won't get home before seven."

When she steered her van out of the lot, David was still standing there, looking startled and satisfactorily guilty.

I'm here. The words echoed once more in her brain, then she stomped on the gas. She was late already.

CHAPTER ELEVEN

IT WAS PAST SEVEN that night by the time Kelly pulled into her drive to find a red pickup parked by the garage. David's truck, she realized.

She found him seated on her deck, his long legs stretched out on the bench before him. "Come see," he whispered, catching her hand.

A skunk waddled across the grass below, its white-plumed tail waving with comical dignity. "Oh!" She laughed under her breath. "And Suki's missing him. We've seen raccoons before, but this is the first skunk."

Cheek to cheek, they watched with quiet pleasure until it nosed off into the twilight. "Where's Suki?" David asked finally.

He'd not yet released her, and she could feel where each of his fingertips rested against her wrist. Did he feel her pulse rushing like a river in springtime? "She's sleeping over with her friend Molly." Not something Kelly would have allowed normally, but this hadn't been a normal month.

"Too bad," David said. "I went out and bought chocolate-chip ice cream for her." He stood and tugged Kelly toward the stairs. "We'll have to eat double helpings to take up the slack."

"What are you talking about?" she asked, hanging back.

"I'm cooking you supper," he announced. "Come to my place and put your feet up while I serve you Whittaker's super-secret spaghetti sauce."

Before she could even frame the words of her refusal, sh
found herself in his truck, backing down the driveway. Wit
a sigh of surrender, Kelly leaned back and closed her eyes
She was in his hands tonight. This should have worried he
Instead, it felt delicious.

David's house was a big, rambling Victorian cottage wit
a wraparound porch overlooking the river. "It's beauti
ful!" she marveled as he led her in through the back.

"I grew up in this house," he told her. "My parent
moved two years ago—retired and went to Florida. I cam
back from California intending to fix it up and sell it fo
them, then found I couldn't do it. Ended up buying it, in
stead. It had been in my mother's family since it was built.'

"Roots..." she murmured dreamily as they entered th
kitchen. "They're nice." That was what she wanted some
day. To put down roots, find a place she and Suki could lov
and cherish. She could certainly see why David cherishe
this place. The kitchen was a warm, old-fashioned roor
with glass-fronted cabinets, work-worn butcher-bloc
counters and a bay window edged with squares of staine
glass.

Someone had modernized the traffic flow by building
work island and by ripping out a wall to gain a view of th
dining room and the river beyond. David's work, she fel
sure. He guided her to a high stool. "Here, sit." He re
turned with a glass of Chianti.

"Can I do anything?" she asked.

"Just talk to me," he said, brushing his knuckles dow
her cheek. But even as she drew back from that caress, h
turned away. "I made the sauce this afternoon," he adde
easily. "All we have to do is boil the spaghetti."

In spite of Kelly's misgivings, he was easy to be with
Conversation flowed, eddied in a pool of comfortable si
lence, then drifted on. He told her he'd flown into Bosto
last night and stayed to show a client some designs ove

breakfast. "I keep forgetting you're an architect," she murmured.

His brows slanted in amusement. "Yes." He disappeared and returned with a set of plans. "These might interest you."

While he made a salad, she spread out the blueprints. "These are the plans for the high school you showed the other night," she observed. She hadn't guessed they were his—had assumed they were part of some contractor's proposal to build the school.

Victoria's cynical words echoed in her brain. . . . *Dummy corporation to bid on the contract . . . they hire our high-minded buddy, David Whittaker, to do the building, and everybody's happy.* And here was the proof to Victoria's suspicions. Kelly stared miserably at the plans. For try as she might, she could see no reason for David to spend hours and hours of his valuable time designing the building if he didn't mean to profit by it in some way.

She might have—just possibly—imagined him working for nothing, if he'd had a child who'd be attending the school. But since he didn't . . . No, he wouldn't have wasted his time on these designs unless he knew for certain that the school committee would choose his plan, no one else's. So Victoria had been right all along—David did have a reason besides altruism to want the new school built.

"What do you think?" David asked while he sliced black olives.

"It's . . . very nice," Kelly murmured without enthusiasm. The building seemed to flow down its hilly site. Part of it would be built underground, yet there appeared to be numerous courtyards and windows, all of which would bring the outdoors inside. Just as he had with the mall, David had obviously based his design on people's needs. Though she didn't know much about architecture, she suspected he was very good.

"It's passive solar to save on heating and cooling," David said, coming to stand beside her. He tapped a row of ragged circles. "These will be flowering cherries. They'll shade the classrooms in summer, then drop their leaves when you want the sun's warmth to penetrate."

"Yes." How much would he earn from this design? she wondered. And if the committee gave him the actual construction contract, as well, he'd make out even better. *Like a bandit.* Victoria would have approved. Tears pricking at the back of her eyes, Kelly looked away. She didn't want to know about his calculating side. She supposed sharp dealing was the way you got ahead in life—Larry would certainly have said so, but still...

They ate in silence. Kelly was too troubled to talk, and David seemed to have concluded she was too tired to be bothered. He wouldn't let her do the dishes after they'd finished. "I'll get them later."

He brewed cups of tea, then led her out onto the porch. He sat in an oak swing that hung from chains, then patted the cushion beside him.

If there had been any other place to sit, she'd have taken it. But the wide porch was bare of furniture. With this view, she'd have wicker chairs out here, maybe a hammock. And there should be climbing roses, trained up the pillars and onto the roof. "Lovely," she murmured, settling on the far end of the swing. At the foot of the yard, a dock jutted into the river. A rowing shell rested on it. So that was how he stayed so fit.

David moved his arm to the backrest behind her. "So tell me about your divorce," he said quietly.

Kelly buried her face in her mug. She sucked in a breath of the lemon-scented steam, then let it out in a sigh. "Not much to tell really—the usual story. I married too young, I guess. He was my boss, back when he was starting his first health-food store, and I just sort of fell into it."

"So he's like you, a granola-and-bean-sprouts type?"

His voice held a note that might have been teasing, but she wasn't sure. She was too tired to challenge it. "No. He was a businessman who saw a new market—health food moving from the fringe into the mainstream—and jumped on the trend. I was the one who took it seriously."

David's fingers curled around her far shoulder. "You take everything seriously," he said, but there was no note of criticism.

She shrugged, very aware of his hand as she did so. "Maybe..."

"And he left you finally?" David asked, stroking her arm.

"Yes, I guess so.... It's a long story."

"Tell me," David commanded, his fingers moving hypnotically.

Kelly slipped lower in her seat till her head rested on David's arm. "Not much to tell really. I'd stopped working in the biz when Suki came. And it had kept on expanding, from one store to two, to a whole chain of them. Then last year, I decided that with Suki in school, I could start working half days again. I'd missed it, you see."

She stared at the black river flowing through the dark. "Soon after I started back, I stumbled on the reason we'd done so well those last few years. Larry was buying nonorganic fruits and vegetables, which cost less, and labeling them organic. The customers were being swindled, paying higher prices for the same produce they could have bought at any grocery store. It...it seemed really awful to me."

"So you told him to stop."

Kelly nodded. "I thought he would. I thought he loved me—and Suki—enough to change." She found that David was drawing her closer. She shouldn't let him, but the warmth of his body against her side was so vastly comforting. She drew a shuddering breath. "Instead of stopping, he sold the stores. Apparently he'd been thinking about it, anyway—my ultimatum was the final straw. I guess I'd have messed up the profit margin, making him stop." She took a final mouthful of tea. "He sold them without even telling me, then he...moved out." She laughed, but it didn't sound like a laugh. "He's gone out to L.A., invested all his money in cellular phones. He'll end up a millionaire before he's done."

"Sounds like you're well rid of him," David said.

Yes. But would admitting that mistake prevent her from making the same sort of mistake again? With the same sort of man? Surely she wasn't that stupid. Her words tumbled out, too brisk, too cheerful, as she sat up and pulled away from him. "Well, it's good to learn I can make it on my own...and I'm loving my freedom. It's so nice to be able to make a decision without having to get a husband's approval. Just decide it and do it—wow! That's a neat feeling."

"Yes, I suppose it must be." David's voice had cooled.

But if they were going to probe so intimately into her life, then Kelly wanted David also to bare himself. "And you, David? You never married?"

"No," David said, and the word was a full stop. He glanced at his watch. "After ten."

Kelly took her cue. "Yes, I should be getting home."

The note of strain, if that's what their silence was, continued as he drove her back. Kelly expected him to simply let her out of the truck, but instead he walked her to her door. "Thanks for cooking for me," she said shyly. She wanted to duck inside, but his gaze held her there.

Slowly his hand rose. Warm fingers curved to fit the side of her throat. "My pleasure," he murmured, not smiling.

He didn't look pleased. He looked almost angry, or perhaps perplexed, as if a sum wouldn't add up the way he thought it should. But he pulled her forward with a gentle, irresistible strength, and she found herself moving into his arms even as she said no.

"No?" He smiled at last and kissed her, a light, warm salute that did not linger. "Oh." The word might have mocked her, might have mocked him, perhaps was meant for them both. "Then sleep tight, Red," he said, his voice rough with some emotion. He squeezed her shoulder and released her. Then he was gone, his steps light and quick on her stairs, before she could think how to reply.

THE THIRD CHILD in the lunch line was so short his bright eyes barely peeked above the tray rails. "There you go, hon," Kelly said, placing a bowl of vegetable beef soup on his tray. Normally Bertie didn't allow her to help on the serving line. But this Friday, the last day of her first week, one of the kitchen workers was out with the flu, which was cutting a swath through the school population. So Kelly had taken her place.

"Yuck! Not that one!" The boy shoved the soup back across his tray. "It's got a hair in it!"

Kelly took the bowl back and checked it. She could see barley, too many lumps of fatty beef, a few washed-out carrots. "I don't see a hair."

"I ain't eating it!" He giggled and elbowed his taller buddy, who was also wriggling with glee. "It's gross!"

Laura Cottrell leaned close and whispered, "He does this every day! Yesterday he claimed there was a fly. Just give him another."

With a swallowed laugh, Kelly gave him a new one. "How's that?"

Apparently this one passed muster, because Mr. Short and Picky slid his tray on toward Mrs. Higgins, who was serving dessert today.

This was Kelly's dessert. Yesterday she'd asked for and received Bertie Higgins's grudging permission to make raisin pumpkin muffins. The kids were receiving two of these with a dollop of apple butter, instead of their usual sugary cupcake plus a white dinner roll with butter.

More fiber and vitamins, less fat, Kelly congratulated herself as she watched the cook plop two of the muffins on a plate.

"What's that?" asked the girl who was being served.

"Just eat it. It's good for you," Mrs. Higgins growled.

The student wrinkled her nose and Kelly rolled her eyes in despair. Didn't Mrs. Higgins know that telling children something was good for them was the kiss of death? Not for the first time, Kelly wished she'd been allowed to serve her own muffins. A strange food had to be offered with enthusiasm and conviction if the children were to accept it.

With a sigh, Kelly ladled out another soup, then another, until she lost count. The kids would love her muffins anyway, she assured herself. What child could resist cinnamon, pumpkin and raisins, even if the recipe in which they came had minimal fat, with egg whites plus yogurt replacing the egg yolks? Bertie would soon see that her ideas weren't so crazy.

But at the end of the lunch period, Mrs. Higgins beckoned Kelly to the garbage can where uneaten food was discarded. The can was full of muffins, most of them untouched, none with more than a bite taken. "Looks like they went over real big!" the woman said with sarcastic glee.

"I don't understand it!" Kelly murmured. She'd tested the recipe at home, then had checked her measurements when she scaled it up for mass production. "Do we have any left?" For health reasons, the head chef forbade sampling while they cooked. So Kelly hadn't tried a muffin from this batch.

"No. After I saw this, I tossed the rest," Mrs. Higgins said with an "I told you so" smirk. "Keep serving them food like that, and we'll have to get a pig to eat all our scraps.'' She bustled off toward the dishwasher.

''Doesn't make sense,'' Kelly muttered as she followed her. Could Bertie have put the kids off by her attitude while she served them?

SHE WAS STILL PUZZLED the next day when she and Suki stopped by the grocery store after work. ''Tell me again what the kids said about the muffins,'' she commanded as they chose a shopping cart.

''Oh, *Mom!*'' Suki moaned. ''I told you they said they tasted funny. Molly threw hers away, then so did the other kids. That's all I remember.''

Suki had brown-bagged as usual and had not noticed that the muffins were her mother's recipe. ''Okay,'' Kelly said, giving up. So her first attempt had been a flop. She'd choose her next recipe carefully, and she'd be darn sure it was she who served it. Consulting her list, she chose an item that Suki could reach on the shelf. ''You run get the olive oil—extra virgin, a gallon. You remember the brand we use?''

''Oh, *Mom!*'' Suki rolled her eyes. She departed at a languid, Mollylike mince, which quickly changed to a hippety-hop. Kelly smiled to herself, then jumped as a hand touched her shoulder.

''You buy real food?'' David stood beside her, his grin belying the gibe.

When she awoke to find the sun shining, it felt like this. ''Of course I do.'' Her own smile felt too broad, but she couldn't seem to moderate it. ''There are lots of products I just can't offer at a competitive price. Not yet, anyway,'' she added wistfully. She glanced at his cart. ''And you, you're planning to live fast, die young? Potato chips? Whole milk?''

''Tastes better,'' David defended himself.

"Cream? Butter? Hot dogs and frozen pizza?" Kelly gave him a pitying look.

"Standard diet of the American bachelor," David agreed, unruffled.

That was exactly what it was. It looked lonely to Kelly, as well as unhealthy, though she doubted David saw it that way. Still, she could have shown him how to make a homemade pizza, loaded with fresh veggies, graced with a minimum of low-fat cheese, that would have knocked his socks off. She stifled the impulse to invite him over and fix him one.

"Here's the—" Suki stopped short beside them, the gallon of oil swinging from one hand. "David!" she cried with unaffected pleasure.

"Hiya, Suki," David said with just the right note of casual warmth. "How's tricks?"

"Oh . . . okay," Suki said, turning mute under his scrutiny. "What else do we need?" she added, swinging to Kelly.

"You're both shy," David observed as he watched her scurry off.

"Only till you get to know us," Kelly replied, rising to Suki's defense.

His keen gray eyes zeroed in on her. "I'd like that," he said simply. "I've been meaning to call you. How about a date?"

"A date?" Kelly echoed foolishly.

"A date," David said. "I'll shine my shoes and wear a jacket. You can— No, don't do anything with your hair. It's great as it is. You could wear that suit you wore when we toured the kitchen."

She wanted to. It hit her as suddenly as if the tower of cereal boxes at her side had toppled over upon her. She couldn't think of anything she'd rather do than date David Whittaker. Even though last week she'd have laughed out loud had someone told her she'd soon want to date any man alive. But what had David once said? Something about the nicest things in life being the ones you tripped over, rather than sought?

Still, even though she wanted to date David, it didn't mean it was the right thing to do. Bitter experience had taught her that she could care for an unscrupulous man. But love for that kind of man was no emotion she could build a life on.

There was no way to tell him she couldn't date him because she found his morals questionable. She needed an excuse. Or perhaps a flat refusal was wiser than any excuse. Certainly it was more honest. "I can't, David."

His smile faded, and his chin came up as if to face a threat. "Can't?" he asked warily. "Or won't?"

Kelly shrugged. "Either... both..." She smiled unhappily. "Please, David, couldn't we just be friends?"

The minute the words left her mouth, she knew they were a mistake. David's expression cooled from searching to remote. "Wasn't exactly what I had in mind," he said dryly. And clearly it wasn't what he wanted. His jaw muscles hardened. "Well, sorry if I've been a nuisance." His strides lengthened till his cart drew ahead.

Kelly watched him go, her teeth bruising her bottom lip. She'd done it all wrong. Said it all wrong. But how could she have said that right?

Suki rounded the end of the aisle as David approached it, and she smiled up at him unguardedly. As the architect passed her, he touched the top of her head with one fingertip in a gentle farewell. He turned the corner with mother and daughter looking after him.

For the first time in months, Kelly felt as if she might cry in public. Blinking her eyes frantically, she turned to stare at three shelves of oversugared cereals.

CHAPTER TWELVE

MONDAY MORNING, all three of the cafeteria workers were out sick, and the substitute that Bertie Higgins called was also down with the flu. "I've never seen it so bad," the cook admitted when she informed Kelly of the disaster. "But it couldn't have happened on a better day. The fifth grade is going to a play in New Bedford. That lets us out of ninety meals."

"We'll manage," Kelly agreed, though she couldn't imagine how.

But the worst was yet to come. At ten, Mr. Tuttle sent a message. Miss Sousa, head of the fifth-grade expedition, had gone home with a temperature. Since another of the field-trip teachers was out sick, as well, this was the crowning blow. The excursion was canceled.

"Ninety more lunches!" Bertie sputtered. "We can't do it!"

But somehow they did. Chopping lettuce and tomatoes with frenzied speed, dashing from the boiling hot dogs, to the baking beans, to the fragrant pans of peanut-butter chewies in the pastry oven, Kelly and the chef somehow cooked a meal for three hundred.

And then they served them all, from sniffling first graders, many of whom clearly should have been home in bed, to fifth graders still sulking about their canceled trip. *And it would be hot dogs!* Kelly groaned to herself as she wedged one frankfurter after another into its white bread bun. She felt utterly wicked, dispensing these pinkish gray, artery-clogging little cylinders to innocent children.

But there was scant time for moral hairsplitting as the first wave of students swept out of the cafeteria and the second wave roared in. "Kelly, we need more chewies!" Bertie boomed, as she dropped another tub of beans into its slot in the serving counter. "And another jar of mustard from the pantry. Please," she added.

Please? Kelly had already dashed into the supply room before the word hit her. Bertie Higgins saying *please* to her worst enemy? With an incredulous laugh, she snatched up the mustard and returned to the fray. Maybe there was a blessing within this disaster, after all.

But if they'd achieved battlefield camaraderie, it waned once the crisis was past. Bertie was almost mute while they cleaned the kitchen. *Or maybe she's coming down with the flu,* Kelly thought, trying to be charitable when the woman stared through the smile she'd just ventured.

Whatever the reason for Bertie's regression, it continued until Kelly dried her hands and looked around. "I guess that's it, then," she said, untying her apron. "I have to relieve my clerk at the store."

"Oh..." The cook seemed about to speak, then she simply grunted in agreement. With a wave, Kelly hurried away.

LATER THAT AFTERNOON at the shop, Kelly looked up from a catalog of vitamins to find Mrs. Higgins standing before her. Kelly blinked. She'd never seen her in anything but aprons and the sacklike housedresses she wore to work. The nicely cut dress Bertie was wearing now mirrored her cornflower blue eyes and brought out a delicate shade of rose in her complexion. Or perhaps those pink cheeks were due to something else.

The cook cleared her throat. "Hi," she said gruffly, and her eyes skated away. She stared around the room. "So, this is your store."

"Yes," Kelly said. "Could I show you around?" Whatever impulse had moved Bertie to come, this was an opportunity not to be missed.

"No! Don't bother!" Bertie snapped. "I came to tell you—" Her face flushed, making her look like an overblown cabbage rose. "I came to tell you that I put salt in your muffin batter last week," she blurted. "About eight cups, when you went to the pantry to get the vanilla."

"Ahh..." Kelly said on a comprehending exhalation. No wonder the kids wouldn't touch the muffins! Her eyes widened as it hit her. Why, of all the underhanded—

"It was a crummy thing to do," Bertie said miserably, echoing her thoughts. "I don't know why I did it."

"I think I do," Kelly said slowly. "It's hard to share a kitchen. Especially with somebody who comes across as a know-it-all in a chicken hat." Her smile mocked herself. "My mother never likes anybody messing around in her kitchen. It's even hard for her to let me lend a hand when I go out and visit her at the health spa where she cooks."

"I thought she died of a heart attack," Bertie said.

"Oh, no, she recovered," Kelly said. "But that was when she had to change her whole way of cooking and eating. We were both terribly overweight. We switched to vegetarian meals to slim down."

"*You* were overweight?" Bertie hooted.

"Sure was," Kelly assured her. "I guess that's why I'm so gung-ho about health food. I know what it's like to eat food that's full of nothing but calories and cholesterol. And it wasn't much fun." And then her eyes met Bertie's and Kelly winced. Lord, if Bertie took her remarks personally...! But before she could stammer out some sort of apology, Elliot Freeling stepped into the store.

At the sight of the cook, the journalist stopped short and drew in his chin like a night heron ducking behind a clump of cattails. "Bertha! I haven't seen you in ages." His eyes darted to Kelly and he managed a wintry smile. "But it looks like I've come at the right time," he added. "I dropped by to ask how your reform campaign's going?"

"Just fine," Kelly said noncommittally. This was all she needed, a newspaperman blundering into the midst of this fragile peace talk!

The journalist turned to Bertie. "And you, Bertha. You're looking in—" he hesitated, then emphasized his next word with acrid gallantry "—*bountiful* health. What do you think about this new program?"

Bertie Higgins drew herself up to her full sixty-one inches and gave him a withering glare. "I keep my thoughts for those who can appreciate them," she said. "I certainly won't go sharing them with a dried-up old stick of a comma-pinching nitpicker—especially one who's dumb enough to think we don't need a new high school around here." She shook her finger at him as he started to speak. "Oh, I read your editorial last week, and you ought to be ashamed of yourself, Elliot! You may think you're smart, but if you'd ever had the brains to get married and have children, you'd know that column was unadulterated hogwash! I almost called you up and told you so." And with that, Mrs. Higgins sailed majestically out of the store.

Kelly bit her lip to keep from laughing. Hats off to Bertie, the clear winner of *this* encounter! Freeling gave himself a shake that reminded Kelly of a bird rearranging its ruffled feathers, then turned back to her with an embarrassed smile. "Well..." he murmured.

"Well, you deserved it," Kelly told him sternly. "That was as nasty a crack as I've heard in quite a while."

"Was it?" He hunched his shoulders, then nodded. "Guess it was. Don't know why I can't keep my mouth shut around her." He turned to stare after the long-vanished Bertha. "She was the prettiest girl in our high-school class...." He shrugged, fished in his pocket for his ever-present notebook and swung back to Kelly. "Well," he said in a voice from which all wistfulness had been driven, "what's the latest?"

KELLY ARRIVED at the cafeteria the next morning unsure whether to expect peace or war. As usual, Bertie was there already, drinking her ritual coffee. Kelly fixed herself a cup and pulled up a stool beside her.

"Elliot get his story?" Bertie growled before Kelly could find a topic.

"He asked a few questions," Kelly said cautiously. "I don't know if he means to write about us this week."

Bertie sniffed. "Maybe not. He'd rather write about trouble."

Meaning there's no trouble here? Kelly hoped. "He was really rude to you," she noted, wondering if she should broach this subject.

A smile lit Bertie's face, giving Kelly a glimpse of the girl Elliot remembered. "He's never forgiven me for not marrying him," she agreed. "He's as proud and stiff-necked as they come."

Kelly nearly choked on her coffee. "He proposed to you?"

The cook nodded. "It would never have worked. He was the smartest boy in our class. I never cracked a book if I could help it—I was too busy dancing and flirting. So I married Ralph Higgins, who was no more a scholar than I was, and I never regretted it. I've five kids and two grandkids to show for it, and I can't remember a quarrel we ever had that lasted till bedtime." She turned the gold band that dented her ring finger. "Ralph passed away two years ago," she said, her eyes misty. Finishing her coffee, she set it down with a smack. "Now if I'd been crazy enough to marry that Elliot, I expect we'd have quarreled three ways to Sunday every day of the week."

"I find him rather...sweet," Kelly ventured.

Bertie chuckled earthily. "Oh, he could be, if he had someone to keep him in line! He needs someone to answer him back when he starts thinking too highly of himself. He was always like that in school. Sort of stuck up and kept to himself. Comes from being shy, to my way of thinking." She smoothed her apron, and her Cupid's-bow mouth turned down. "Still, that was a mean thing to say." She sighed. "I always say I put on ten pounds for each of the children, but it's the cooking that really does it. How about your mother? If she cooks for a living, she isn't gaining it back?"

Kelly shook her head. "It's almost impossible to gain weight on a low-fat vegetarian diet. Beans and rice and veggies make you feel satisfied, but they just don't have enough calories to fill you out."

"That so?" Bertie gave a soft grunt as she got to her feet. "How's it for losing weight?"

"It worked for us," Kelly said simply. "That and walking two or three miles every day, rain or shine." She finished her own coffee and stood. "The secret is not to worry or even think about losing weight," she confided. "You just focus on treating yourself right—cooking the healthiest, tastiest meals you can. And you focus on how wonderful it feels to be outside, using your body. The rest just comes naturally."

Bertie looked skeptical. "But how long does it take?"

"You don't worry about that," Kelly insisted. "You just enjoy each day as it comes, and before you know it, it's not an issue anymore."

Bertie's snort dismissed the topic, then she turned to consult the wall clock. "Well, things shouldn't be quite so crazy today. Laura says she's coming in, and I've drafted my daughter Emily to help out."

With those reinforcements, the morning went smoothly, even though Emily had to bring in her nine-month-old daughter, because her sitter was also down with the flu. But the child slept in her stroller in the pantry, oblivious to the clatter of pots in the adjacent kitchen.

The day went well for Kelly, too. Halfway through it Bertie asked her to plan the Thursday and Friday meals. And from now on she was to be in charge of desserts, if she thought she could handle it. "No problem!" Kelly assured her, her eyes sparkling. With Bertie no longer fighting her, she knew she could sell the kids on her recipes.

Just as the first wave of students rushed in to be served, Elliot Freeling poked his beaky nose through the back door. "Mind if I come in and watch?" he called to Bertie, who'd taken her place in the serving line.

"Stirring up trouble, are you?" Bertie scowled at him, then swung toward the pantry as a baby's wail rose above the din from the outer room. "No, Emily, I need you," she added imperiously, as the child's mother left her place at the mashed potatoes. The cook jerked her head at Elliot. "If you want to hang around, then make yourself useful," she commanded. "Go see what's wrong with that baby."

Kelly watched as a look of sheer panic crossed the journalist's face. Then she turned back to find Mr. Short and Picky bouncing on his tiptoes as he waited to find something wrong with today's menu.

She didn't have time to look again until the first shift was served. When she did, Kelly found the journalist pacing the kitchen, a contented baby pressed to his bony shoulder. Elliot wore an expression of harassed pride—as if he were the first to make the discovery that babies liked rhythmic movement and body heat.

The next time Kelly checked, she found Elliot looking more dismayed than proud while Bertie scrubbed at a damp spot on his shirt where the baby had spit up. Hiding her grin, Kelly stacked the empty serving tubs. Maybe there was hope for Elliot yet.

KELLY'S OWN HOPES of forgetting David and getting on with her life were not so easy to fulfill. She had not heard a word from the architect since their encounter at the grocery store.

Perversely, she found that there was nobody she'd rather hear from. It didn't seem to matter that she still thought she'd done the right thing by refusing to date him. As one day passed, then two, she found herself running for the phone each time it rang, looking up with a hopeful smile each time a man with a jaunty walk passed her store. The second night, she actually picked up the phone and started to dial. She'd said she wanted to be friends, after all. Friends were allowed to call one another, weren't they? But she put the phone down again. David could hardly want to hear from her. His echoing absence from her life should tell her that.

When she did have news of David at last, it came from an unexpected source. Mr. Tuttle dropped by the kitchen for "a little inspection tour," as the principal called his midmorning raids on their refrigerator. Munching on a cold piece of the vegetarian pizza they'd served the day before, he admitted to Kelly, "Not bad at all, though me, I like my pizza with extra cheese." He took another bite, swallowed and added, "So does your friend Whittaker. Saw him at Mario's last night. He took home four deluxes."

"Having a party," Kelly ventured with a smile that hid a stab of pain.

"Uh-uh." Tuttle crammed the last bite into his mouth. "S'coming down with the blasted flu. Said he was laying in supplies so he wouldn't have to cook." He headed back to the refrigerator. "That prune-apple cobbler you girls served yesterday. Any of that left?"

David had said that friendship wasn't what he had in mind. But a friend in need is a friend indeed, Kelly reminded herself a few hours later. Holding a canvas grocery bag that contained a bottle of vitamin C, an herbal tea that was good for sore throats and a quart of her own special frozen yogurt, she knocked on his front door. No answer. Getting the same result at the back door, she finally opened it and leaned inside. "David?"

Somewhere overhead she could hear music, what sounded like a saxophone. So he must be awake. "David?" she called again as she started up the stairs.

She found him asleep in bed, a writing pad propped on his bare chest, a pen clutched in one hand. On the bedside table, an untouched pizza sat in its box—the supper he'd not been able to stomach, she supposed.

Next to the box, a silver picture frame held a photo of a laughing girl. *California girl,* Kelly thought, noting the bleached hair and the skimpy bikini, though she seemed too young for David. Perhaps this was a memento from his college days? Across the big, airy room, a compact-disc player supplied the music she'd heard. "David," she said again, coming to sit on the edge of the bed.

His chest glistened with sweat, she noted in alarm, and his face was flushed bright with fever. In spite of his day's growth of beard, he looked incredibly young with his hair tousled. His dark lashes drifted up when she set her palm to his forehead. "Kelly...what are you doin' here?"

"Checking on you," she said severely. "Where's your thermometer?"

"Don't have one." Catching her wrist, he dragged her hand down to his cheek, then closed his eyes again. "I must be dreaming...."

Unexpectedly, tears stung her eyes. "Nope," she said, her voice too brisk and cheerful. With her free hand, she pulled the thermometer she'd brought from her bag, flicked off its top and shook it.

"Your hand's cold," David murmured dreamily as he accepted it.

"That's your fever." She set his pad aside. "What are you writing?"

David pulled the thermometer from his mouth. "Letter o the *Dartmouth Daily.* Elliot keeps slamming our need for a new school. And Leland Howard wrote another letter to he editor against it. Somebody's got to answer them. Make people see the other side."

Kelly guided the thermometer back to his lips. "Did you eat today?" When he shook his head, she sniffed. "That's what I figured. Keep that under your tongue till I come back."

David had a fever of 102, Kelly discovered when she re-urned with a bowl of frozen yogurt. The only good thing about that was that he was too feeble to resist her ministra-ions. She'd spooned half the yogurt down him before he hought to growl, "What is this stuff?"

She got another bite down him before answering. "Fro-zen yogurt mixed with whipped tofu, bananas, wheat germ, honey and kiwi fruit."

"Aaagh!" He made a face. "Couldn't I just have ice cream?"

"And miss out on all this protein and vitamin C and po-assium?" She nudged another spoonful against his lips. "Trust me, your body needs this."

"Maybe that's what it needs, but it's not what it wants." His fever-bright eyes gleamed at her over the spoon.

I suppose I asked for that, she thought as her cheeks warmed. There was something so intimate about caring for him like this. It wasn't her proximity to his half-naked body,

though that was overwhelming enough. To her it was mor
an emotional bonding. Somehow you came to feel posses-
sive about what or whom you cared for, in the same way
she'd always felt a protective passion for each sprout an
seedling in her garden. By responding to his need today
she'd accepted a small stake in his life and his happiness.

"Sorry," he said when she didn't respond. "Blame it o
the fever."

"Sure." But suddenly they were too close, the urge t
brush her hand through the dark, curly hair on his chest too
strong. She put the bowl in his hands and stood. "Who's th
girlfriend?" she teased, nodding at the photo. Friends wer
allowed to be nosy, she assured herself.

"M'daughter," he muttered around a spoonful of yo
gurt. "Sunshine."

Kelly forgot her pose of indifference. "Your daughter!
thought you'd never married?"

David's ears grew pink to match his feverish cheeks
"That's right," he said coolly, and put the reloaded spoo
back in his mouth.

Sore point, Kelly realized as he glared at a spot over he
shoulder. *Major sore point.* "Oh . . ."

"She lives in California with her mother," he added, an
the flatness of his tone signaled the end to this topic.

"Oh," Kelly said, smothering a hundred questions. Sh
turned away, giving him time to recover. But who had re
fused to marry whom? she wondered. Or had neither par
ent wanted to formalize the association? And who, for pity'
sake, had chosen the name Sunshine? She'd never dare ask
and apparently David didn't volunteer information on thi
subject. "What are you playing?" she asked at random
wandering across the room.

"Bill Evans. Some early Miles . . ."

"Oh," she murmured, her eyes coming to rest on his bi
desk, where the plans for the new school were spread out a

f he'd been studying them. She felt a wave of unhappiness wash over her. She kept forgetting those plans. But David sure wasn't forgetting—witness that letter he was drafting. She let out a sigh between her teeth.

Why let it matter? she asked herself. *I'm not in charge of his honesty.* If he was only a friend, then let him look to his own conscience. But still, the radiance had gone from her day, the way the light dims when a cloud crosses the sun. She turned. "I've got to run, David, I'm due at the store. But I've left more of this yogurt in your freezer, and there's some herb tea on the counter. Do you think you'll be all right?" She paused by his bed.

"I'm better already," he assured her, not looking better at all. Reaching out, he touched her hand with his hot fingers. "Thanks."

"Sure... friend." She swung back in his doorway to give him one last smile, and a shaft of pain shot through her. Whether he knew it or not, he needed someone to care for him. Everyone did. If she hadn't had Suki's health to worry about, she'd have simply bundled him into her car and settled him on her couch until he was well again. She sighed. "Take care," she said softly, and hurried out the door.

CHAPTER THIRTEEN

IF KELLY THOUGHT she'd been busy before, it was nothin compared to her schedule the next week. But if her day were hectic, they were also satisfying.

At school, she oversaw the gradual infiltration of vege tarian meals into the lunch program. They served vegetabl lasagna on Friday, bean burritos on Monday. Far fron balking at the food, the kids cleaned their plates. Kell doubted if one in ten noticed they were enjoying meatless low-fat cooking, and that was fine with her. Healthy eatin shouldn't be intrusive, after all. It should be a habit as pur and simple as breathing.

When she wasn't cooking or working in the shop, sh juggled her need to be with Suki and her concern for Da vid. Each evening when they walked, they walked to Da vid's house. He was mending slowly. The fever broke afte three days, but it left him weak and prone to nasty head aches.

Even so, he was good company. They fell into the habi of sitting on his back porch, drinking cups of tea and tell ing him about their day while the sun set over the river an the rabbits came to dance on his lawn.

And if David still entertained any notions other tha friendship, he kept them to himself, which was fine by Kelly Freed from pressure to be more than she could be to him she found her heart lifting at first sight of his face. Sh found herself bringing him gifts—a blue-jay feather she' found, a magazine article, a slice of the high-protein cheesecake she'd served the kids that day, the latest gossip.

"You think *you* were mad about Tuesday's editorial against the new school," she said with a laugh on Wednesday. "You should have seen Bertie tear into Elliot! She actually grabbed him by his necktie and shook him, she was so mad."

"Good for her." David tipped Kelly's Red Sox cap up so that he could see her eyes. "What did she say?"

"She..." For a second, Kelly's words evaporated while David's eyes looked into hers, then she found her voice. "She asked him why he didn't do something constructive with his life, rather than tear things down. Her older grandchild will be starting high school next year, and she's hopping mad that he'll be on double sessions."

"So she should be," David agreed. "What did Elliot say?"

"Not much," Kelly admitted, "but I think he was hurt. I think he's really sweet on Bertie, if you want to know the truth. He's been stopping by almost daily on some pretty flimsy excuses."

"Wouldn't surprise me," David said, not smiling now. "She's a whole lot of woman." He reached for Kelly's cap again and this time lifted it off her head. "As are you," he added quietly.

David's friendship was coming to mean too much to her—and she couldn't let him risk it this way. "Joke about my height at your peril, bud!" she teased, socking him on the shoulder as she stepped past him. "Sukums, we'd better hit the road. I don't want to walk home in the dark."

When she looked back, David still stood on his porch, smacking her forgotten cap against his thigh. She waved, but he was a long time in waving back.

AFTER HIS CHASTISEMENT, Elliot stayed out of Bertie's kitchen for more than a week before reappearing with a strange man in tow. "I was wondering if we could buy lunch?" he asked Bertie, his gaunt cheeks actually going pink under her unbending gaze.

Bertie looked the journalist and his companion up and down, then shrugged. "If you've got nothing better to do."

Kelly hid a smile as she eavesdropped shamelessly. Elliot couldn't have chosen a better day to please Bertie. They were serving a meal that the cook had devised—a bean, corn and tomato casserole topped with corn bread, a tossed salad garnished with whole-wheat croutons and pumpkin seeds, a scoop of frozen banana yogurt for dessert. Kelly let out a contented sigh. If Bertie was going to start putting meals like that together on a regular basis, then her work was nearly done. She could get back to her own badly neglected life, and Suki could start buying her meals at the cafeteria like all the other children.

"Great..." Elliot shuffled his feet. "Great. I, er, saw you out walking early the other morning...."

"Did you?" Bertie's clear Irish complexion went a shade rosier.

"Er, yes...and..." Elliot tugged at his tie as if to loosen it. "Uh, have you done something to your hair, Bertha?"

She was taking more care with it, but Kelly bet that wasn't the change Elliot was sensing. Bertie was eating strictly low-fat now, and she'd lost four pounds. If the weight loss didn't show in her face yet, there was a new aura of hope and vitality that made her glow. But most likely it was Elliot's bumbling attentions that were making that difference.

"What if I have?" Bertie sniffed. In spite of her apparent disdain, she took extra care with the plates she filled for Elliot and his friend.

"And she garnished Elliot's plate with a radish cut like a rose," Kelly told her mother that evening during their weekly phone call.

Helen chuckled. "She'll be fixing him breakfast before she knows it. But what about your man, sweetie?"

"I've *told* you, Mom, we're just friends," Kelly protested.

Helen made a wordless sound of disbelief.

"He's still pushing like crazy for his new high school," Kelly added with a sigh. "He actually bought a half-page ad in the local paper, urging people to vote for it in two weeks at the Financial Town Meeting."

"That must have cost him plenty," Helen observed.

"If he gets to build the new high school, he'll make it back, believe me," Kelly said with a touch of bitterness.

"You really think he's another Larry?" Helen asked gently.

"I don't know," Kelly moaned, unable to hide the misery in her voice. "I can't sort it out. When I'm with him, when I look at him, I think no, David would never do anything sneaky or underhanded. Never. But when we're apart, I remember that his father used his political connections to pull this same sort of scam. And I remember that David has the school already designed and waiting. And I wonder why someone with no kids in the district would be so... so passionate about wanting this school built."

"Well, there's one sure way to sort it out," Helen said brightly. "Wait. The election's only two weeks away. And if the bond passes, I expect they'll start taking bids for a contractor immediately, won't they?"

"And once the contract is awarded, then I'll know," Kelly concluded. *For better or worse.* "You make it sound so simple."

"And once you're satisfied that he's not like Larry, you pounce," her mother advised mischievously.

"Nope," Kelly said, and let out an exasperated breath. "
do not. Honestly, Mom, we're just friends." Before David
she'd never known how much a friendship could matter.

"DID YOU SEE THIS?" he demanded a week later, waving a
magazine at Kelly the minute she walked in his door. He'd
invited her to an early supper. Kelly had hesitated before
accepting—she'd noticed a certain gleam returning to David's eyes lately, which had made her nervous. But she'd
sensed that he especially needed a friend tonight. The schoo
committee would be presenting its school budget to the town
council in a special session at eight, and David was clearly
keyed up. Without the town council's active backing for the
school-construction bond, the voters would surely reject it
next week.

"No. What is it?" Accepting the periodical, she found it
was the supplement that came each Sunday with the *Boston Globe*. David had folded it to an article entitled
"School Lunches: Healthy or Hazardous?" On the facing
page, a photo showed Bertie, Kelly and Laura serving lunch
to a line of students. "Who took this?" she gasped.

"The guy who wrote the article. He's the *Globe*'s restaurant critic."

"Elliot brought him to lunch!" she exclaimed as she
scanned the feature. "But we didn't notice him taking pic-
tures." Had Elliot done this to show Bertie he could be
constructive? "Gosh, he says our food measured up to
meals he's eaten in some of Boston's best vegetarian restau-
rants!"

"He had some nice things to say about you, too." David
brushed a wisp of hair out of her eyes.

"Yes," she agreed without looking up. The writer praised
her efforts and mentioned her store, but she was glad to see
that his main focus was on the meals themselves and the
need to improve school lunches in general.

The article went on to compare Kelly's pilot program to the standard cafeteria lunches of a neighboring school district. Then it compared them both to the health-conscious fare presented at the private school across town, where money was apparently no object. "Why, this is my landlord's daughter!" She held up a photo that showed Stephanie Howard filling a sugar cone at a frozen-yogurt machine. "And it says their cafeteria is run by a nutritionist. It has an unbelievable salad bar, daily choices of meat, fish or vegetarian..." She shook her head in wonder.

"Yeah, but if they'd put a little of that money back into the public schools, instead, then maybe kids wouldn't be picking falling plaster out of their lunches in the cafeteria at the high school," David growled.

While Kelly finished the article, David brought the food out to a table he'd set on the porch. "I'm afraid it's pretty basic," he warned. "I meant to do something extra special tonight, but Ellen May and I've been wrapping up the budget all day. There was lots of last-minute number crunching."

"This looks wonderful," Kelly assured him, as he set out a platter of boiled shrimp arranged on ice, a loaf of Italian bread fresh from the oven, a Caesar salad and a split of—"Champagne?" She looked up, startled.

"Why not? It's spring at last and I like the company." David popped the cork and filled their glasses, then lifted his. "To... a most determined young woman," he teased, quoting the magazine article.

"To..." She'd meant to toast his hopes for the new school, but at the last second, she couldn't. It still bothered her.

"To new beginnings?" David suggested.

She wasn't sure what beginnings he was thinking of, but she nodded and sipped, then caught her breath in an appreciative gasp. It was like drinking moonlight. Like a fingertip brushing down her spine.

They ate, sharing the warm, lighthearted companionship that had grown between them over the past few weeks. *We know each other so well, and yet we don't know each other at all,* Kelly thought, listening to him tell a story. She'd guarded her heart from the start, and David had responded in kind, not trusting her with his deepest and most painful secrets. But she could see them lurking behind his eyes sometimes—tonight, for instance.

"Penny for 'em?" David asked, smiling at the serious look on her face.

She shook her head. They'd reached a perfect balance of friendship and independence. To delve deeper was to risk undermining the whole relationship. *I was thinking you were a wonderful friend,* she told him silently, *and that I couldn't bear to lose you.*

"I'll tell you mine then," he said, reaching to take her hand.

He'd not touched her in weeks, not romantically, anyway, and she sucked in a breath. Warm and gentle, his fingers curled around hers, and she felt a flicker of panic. *Oh, David, don't!*

"I know you said you just want to be friends." His voice grew huskier. "So I've been trying to respect that these past few weeks, Kelly. And it's been good—very good. Having you for a friend has made me realize how much I like you, apart from all else. Even if you *are* a little intense about bean sprouts."

The last sentence was delivered on a lighter note, then he grew serious again. "But it's not enough, Kelly. It isn't all that I want, and I don't think it's enough for you, either. I want to make love to you. I'd be crazy if I didn't." His fingers tightened as she tried to draw away, then he let go, but his eyes held her fast. "So, I'd like you to release me from that understanding, Kelly. I want to court you. I'll go slow, if that's what you want, but that's where I'm headed—toward you and me together. I'd be lying if I let you think otherwise."

She'd had only one glass of champagne, but now she wished she hadn't. Her thoughts were spinning, just when she needed them straight and clear. Somehow she had to cut through this panic, not hurt him with her words. But all she could think was that he'd betrayed her. This was what had been growing behind his eyes while she'd thought she was safe with him. "I can't, David. I'm just not ready."

"You still love him?" David asked, his words grating. "It doesn't sound like he deserves—"

"No, it's not Larry at all!" she insisted, standing and going to the railing. "It's that..." It was so many things, most of all the question of David's honesty, but that she could never say. She'd just have to wait and see. "It would never work," she said without conviction. "A carnivore like you and an enlightened kelp-eater like me?" She smiled to underline the joke.

"'You say potato and I say potahto'?" David quoted as he joined her. "I don't buy that, Kelly. We can meet somewhere in the middle, like we're doing tonight, eating shrimp." His hand covered hers on the railing. "Or we'll cook to please both of us. There's room in my fridge for tofu as well as T-bone." His fingers curled around hers. "And I don't care what kind of crackers you eat in bed, low-fat or high-fat, as long as you eat them in *my* bed."

For a second, an image of domestic bliss lighted her mind. The two of them lying in bed together, propped on pillows, his arm around her shoulders, their feet laced together, an old film on the TV set at the foot of the bed, her whole-wheat crackers forgotten on the bedside table.

Gently she pulled her hand away. "David, it's not just that. It's... it's that for the first time in my life, I'm growing . . ." She shook her head, groping for the words to make him see. "Maybe it sounds stupid, but I'm *blossoming*. I'm learning to do things I thought I could never do—run a shop, support myself and Suki doing it, make friends, make a school district listen to me when I know it's important. . . ." She laughed shakily. "Don't you see? My marriage was like a box. I'm so afraid that . . ."

"That marrying me would put you back in the box?" David's laugh was harsh and incredulous. "You think I'd do that to you?"

Did she? She'd feared so for a while, but now? She was stronger than she'd dreamed, and he was kinder. And too sure of himself to need to crush her personality as Larry had. Her strength would never threaten his. "No," she admitted softly. "No, you wouldn't."

"Well, then, what's the problem?" David demanded, reaching to recapture her hand.

At bedrock the problem was that she couldn't, wouldn't let herself love him, not while she had the tiniest doubt about his honesty. She looked away from his searching eyes. Out on the twilit lawn, two rabbits grazed, their noses almost touching. That was what David wanted, wasn't it? And how could she blame him for that when she wanted the same thing? "David, I can't date you seriously," she pleaded as he put a finger to her chin and turned her to face him. "I just can't. Not yet." If only he'd waited. She was only weeks from knowing the truth.

But as his frown deepened, a wave of panic swept through her. "B-but if you wanted to date in an *un*serious way . . ." she added reluctantly. She'd do that, if that was what it took to keep his friendship. The thought of losing it was unthinkable. And she'd have time to find out why he was so determined to build the new school, and if she could live with his motives.

"In an unserious way?" he echoed, looking as if he'd swallowed something sour.

"No strings attached," she clarified.

He snatched his hand away. "No, thanks," he said bitterly. "I've been offered a deal like that before. Believe me, there are always strings attached."

"But there wouldn't be!" she insisted, stung. "That's what I'm trying to tell you. It would just be dating with a small *d*."

"And what I'm trying to tell you is that's the *last* thing I want!" David snarled. "No way will I let you play with my heart. I'm not playing, Kelly. I don't want love with a small *l*. I'm serious, and if you aren't, and if you can't be, then...then to hell with it!" Spinning on his heel, he stalked down the steps to the lawn, sending the rabbits bolting for the bushes. He jammed his hands into his pockets and headed off toward the river.

Eyes misted with tears, she stood there paralyzed. Half of her wanted to run and throw herself into his arms, to beg his forgiveness and swear she'd do anything he wanted, anything at all, if he'd still be her friend. The other half of her, as always, held back. Fear kept her pinned to the safety of the porch. Finally, with a heartfelt sigh, she carried their dishes to the kitchen.

When she came back, he'd returned, but his face was as remote as the sliver of moon in the fading sky. "I'm sorry I lost it like that," he said, his voice cool. "And thanks for your offer, but I don't want a half-serious love affair. I don't want an affair at all. So let's just skip it, shall we?"

She'd won, and lost everything by winning, she realized, nodding miserably. Their friendship wouldn't survive this. Neither of them had gotten what they wanted.

David glanced at his watch. "It's too late to walk to the meeting. Why don't we take separate cars in case I stay late?"

So they made their own way to the high school. Onc there, David sat on the stage with the other school-com mittee members, off to one side of the presiding tow council, while Kelly sat in the audience, her arms wrappe tight around the ache in her middle.

She might as well have been sitting in Timbuktu. Diml she was aware that the town council was dealing with cru cial budget matters, but her own thoughts spun crazil around what she could have said, should have done. O stage, David also seemed to be scowling into space.

When she finally did focus on the proceedings, she foun that, after two hours of wrangling, the town council ha accepted the school committee's budget for next year. Sh drew a shaky breath. That left only the matter of the ne high school. If the town council seconded the school com mittee in asking that the voters approve the bond issue t build the school, the bond had a good chance of passage But if the council refused to support it, the bond would al most surely be voted down at the town meeting next week.

"Leland Howard's the key," David had told her at sup per. The head of the town council opposed the new hig school. "But if he decides enough voters want it, he'll try t get out ahead and lead them that way. Whichever way h jumps, you can bet the rest of the town council will fol low."

Her eyes moved to Leland to find he was beaming at her "But before we move on to the high-school constructio bond," he said into his microphone, "I'd like to give som recognition to an *outstanding* citizen. I'm sure you all kno that Ms. Bouchard has volunteered to improve the meals a Oake Elementary?" He waited for the audience's murmur of assent to die, then continued. "Those of you who rea the *Boston Globe* will know. . ." He went on to describe th favorable publicity that Kelly had brought the town, notin that the students, teachers and even Mrs. Higgins and he workers loved the changes Kelly had implemented. And that with Kelly's help, Mrs. Higgins was going to revise the menus for the entire school district next fall. "So, Ms. Bouchard, would you please stand so that we may give you our sincerest thanks for a job well done?"

This was the last thing Kelly wanted, but there was no escaping it. She stood, blushed tomato red while the audience gave her a hearty round of applause, then dropped back into her seat, not daring to look at David.

The town-council president was still speaking. "I think we could all take a page from Kelly Bouchard's notebook. Kelly's an example of what West Dartmouth needs—the spirit of volunteerism. The resolve to pinch pennies and make do. Kelly is living proof that problems can be solved by other ways than just throwing money at them!"

His voice grew more intense, as if his speech had just turned some hidden corner. "And so," he said suavely, "I'd like to urge that the school committee approach the question of a new school in the same spirit as Kelly Bouchard approached her problem. We don't *need* an expensive new building, people of West Dartmouth! What we need are teachers and administrators *with the grit, and will, and imagination of Kelly Bouchard!* People who are willing to roll up their sleeves and find a solution to this problem that won't bankrupt the town. So I urge you all to vote next week *against* the bond to build a new high school. And though I haven't discussed this with my fellow committee members, I'm sure they'll..."

Leland said more, but Kelly no longer listened. She was staring at David in openmouthed horror. He'd been right, every step of the way! Leland had used her. Used her first as a red herring to distract the voters from the issue of the new school. And now he was using her as proof that a new school was not needed at all. Bare-knuckled fighting didn't begin to describe Leland's tactics. A knife in the back was more accurate! *David will never forgive me!* The roaring in her ears almost drowned out the sounds of the town council, as they unanimously recommended that the voters reject the school bond at the annual town meeting one week hence. All she could hear were David's words. *He's using you, Kelly.* All she could see was David's rigidly controlled face, with the telltale knots where his jaw muscles had clenched.

Once the town council had voted, David requested permission to speak. "On behalf of the school committee," he said, his voice raw with suppressed anger, "I can only say that we hope the people of West Dartmouth have more brains and more concern for their own children than their town council does. A new high school is *desperately* needed. Has been for four years. I invite you all to walk through this building before you leave tonight. If you do, then you'll see for yourself. And I ask you—no, I beg you—to vote accordingly.

"Meanwhile—" he bowed his head for a second, then lifted it to stare out over the audience "—I've worked for two years on behalf of this new school. That's not as long as many of the other school-committee members, but I'm afraid it's all the time I can stomach, given the attitude we're up against in this town. So I hereby resign. Thank you, and I wish your children good luck." He walked offstage and disappeared into the wings.

While the audience rumbled their shock, Kelly sat dumbfounded, her heart trying to pound its way through the top of her head. *Oh, David, this is all my fault!* Then she sprang to her feet.

As she tore out of the building, the headlights of David's truck swept across the parking lot. But the road led past the school's front steps, and she dashed into the middle of the pavement, her arms spread wide.

With a squeal of brakes, his truck came to a halt before her. "Out of the way!" he called.

"David, please!" she panted, running to his window. "Oh, please—"

"Kelly, I can't talk to you," he said with deadly calm. "Go away."

"David, I'm so sorry!" she blurted. "You were right from the very start, and I was wrong, and I'm so terribly sorry!"

"Lot of good that does the kids now," he said. "Or us."

The awful finality of those two quiet words set loose her tears. He was right, but still... "Why do you care so much?" she sobbed. "I mean, of course it's a good cause, but why take it so to heart? Why make it yours? Do you need the business that much?"

"Business?" He stared at her. "What are you talking about?"

"You've already designed the damn thing!" She swiped at her eyes. "You mean to build it if it ever gets approved, don't you?"

"You think I've been working for this just so I could get the contract?" David's voice cracked with outrage. "That's illegal, or if it isn't, it's damn sure immoral! You've never heard of conflict of interest, lady?"

She'd made a horrible mistake. The note of stark incredulity in his voice told her so. "B-b-but you did the plans. Why would you—"

"To save the town *money*, that's why! I designed it for free. That saves us the architect's fees. And I did it because nobody could do the job better than I can."

"Oh, David—"

"And I did it because I thought—I hoped—I could persuade Sunshine to come live with me for her high-school years," he added bleakly. "But I couldn't ask her to come if I didn't have a decent school to offer her, and I don't believe in private schools." He shook his head and kept on shaking it. "You've had some opinion of me from the start, haven't you?" He laughed, but there was no humor in the sound. "You're just like the rest of them, thinking, like father, like son. I don't know why I ever thought I could come back to this town. I was an idiot to even try."

"David—" she touched his arm "—David, I'm so sorry. I've been a fool, thinking you could ever... I guess it's because my ex-husband would have..."

He jerked his arm away from her fingers. "Yeah? Well, someday, Kelly, you'd better learn to tell the jerks from the good guys." He eased the truck into motion. When he was sure she'd stepped out of the way, he stomped on the gas. The truck was still accelerating when it vanished beyond the trees.

So there was nothing to do but go home and cry. Kelly didn't even make it home. Halfway there, she had to pull off the road and weep for a while. When she started the van again, she drove instead to David's house. She didn't know what more she could say, but she couldn't leave things like this.

His home was dark, and the truck was not in the driveway. He was out walking off his fury on some beach, she guessed. But she hadn't time to search for him. She'd promised Suki's sitter she'd be home by eleven, and it was almost twelve.

Lisa, the sitter, was asleep on the couch when Kelly let herself in. She sat up and rubbed her eyes. "Some man called," she mumbled. "Forgot his name. Said to tell you goodbye, he's gone back to California."

"That's all?" Kelly almost shook the girl. "Nothing else?"

"S'all I remember," the teenager muttered, and went to find her purse.

CHAPTER FOURTEEN

"BUT HE'S GOT to come back," Victoria insisted when Kelly dragged herself into work the next afternoon. "He owns a house here. Though I suppose he could have some realtor sell it for him."

That wasn't what Kelly wanted to hear. She wanted to hear that David would come back from California, that he'd give her another chance.

To do what? she wondered. He'd offered her his heart, and she hadn't accepted. Was she such an idiot that she'd decide she really wanted him, now that she'd ruined everything? She swallowed the lump in her throat.

"He'll be back," Victoria assured her, as she opened Kelly's copy of the *Globe* magazine. "Hey, this is a great article!"

Kelly stared at the photo of Stephanie Howard and her frozen-yogurt machine. How easy it would be to convert the kids at Oake Elementary to healthy eating with goodies like that! The first flicker of anger cut through her sorrow as she remembered the private school's state-of-the-art juicer that turned out fresh carrot juice, the nutritionist, the marvelous salad bar. Why, Leland's daughter had every advantage money could buy!

And yet the town-council president and his allies were doing everything in their power to block the sorely needed public high school. David had every right to be angry. Such tactics were cynical and stingy, as well as lacking foresight.

Worst of all, Leland had used *her* to help him achieve his selfish ends.

Kelly clenched her teeth. *Not if I can help it!* She might have wrecked her chance for happiness with David. But she was darned if she was going to let Howard use her to wreck David's hopes for a decent education for the kids of West Dartmouth. She owed David that much, and she owed the kids of the town that much. Whatever damage she'd done, she was going to repair—somehow. "If I can convert Bertie Higgins to cooking with tofu," she muttered, "then I can do anything."

But could she work a miracle in the one week that remained before the annual town meeting?

MIRACLES TAKE TIME, so the first thing Kelly did was offer Jane double pay to run Pure and Simple from opening till closing. Luckily her assistant was delighted to comply. And Kelly would just have to worry about the gaping hole that blew in her budget later.

Miracles take manpower. Kelly meant to contact every voter in West Dartmouth that week, but she couldn't do it alone. She needed foot soldiers. Well, she had the names and phone numbers of 180 civic-minded parents from her original petition. And Bertie and Laura offered to help after work, when she told them of her plan. So did Ellen May from the school committee and a dozen other supporters of the new school she put Kelly in touch with. By nightfall, Kelly had recruited forty people willing to go door-to-door.

A miracle needs a focus—that was easy. Kelly copied the photos in the *Boston Globe* article. "At each house you go to, show them this," she told her troops when they met outside Pure and Simple that evening. "This is the kind of school Leland Howard's daughter attends. Yet he doesn't want the same advantages for the kids of West Dartmouth? The voters need to come out and tell him where to get off!

Who says our kids don't deserve a super education and the building to get it in?"

A miracle needs publicity. "Leave that to me!" Bertie announced. "Elliot's going to come out on our side, or I'll know the reason why!" And whatever she said to the journalist, it worked. The lead editorial in the next edition of the *Daily* came out staunchly in favor of the new high school. Elliot also wrote a story about Kelly's campaign itself. For a side article he brought in a private building inspector to survey the old high school, and that man wrote a scathing indictment of the building's deficiencies. Most amazing of all, Elliot joined Bertie in the door-to-door campaign—and smiled while he did it.

A miracle takes courage. Elliot arranged for Kelly and Ellen May to speak on a local talk-radio program. Kelly was terrified of the microphone, and the thought of all those people out there listening made her sick to her stomach, but she did it, anyway. With her courage hat pulled down around her ears, she fielded phone-in questions, comments and even insults from listeners. "And I didn't make a *total* fool of myself," she told Victoria when she stopped by the mall after the show. *What would David have thought of me?* she wondered. *Would he have been proud?* But that thought led to too much heartache, so she set it aside. She had no time to mope if she was going to work a miracle.

And miracles always mean sacrifice. "You're showing photos of my kid around town?" her landlord stormed when he came to her door on the third day. "And you know how I feel about this new school—it'll raise property taxes. It's not needed."

Kelly drew herself up to her full height, which put her eyeball-to-eyeball with Howard. "Not needed? Don't make me laugh, Leland!"

"We'll see who laughs last!" he snarled, shaking a finger in her face. "You're out of here, Kelly, if you don't stop this nonsense! Quit this door-to-door whining, or move out. Make your choice."

"I have," Kelly said. "We'll move at the end of the month if that's how you feel." After he'd stomped off, she stood for a while on the deck, staring sadly at her bird feeder. Then she squared her shoulders. Somehow she thought David would have cheered her stand—if he'd cared at all.

And finally, after all the work and the persuasion and the hope and the time and the sacrifice, miracles take caring. *Do the people of West Dartmouth care enough about their children to pay for their education?* Kelly wondered as she took the seat Bertie had saved for her in the school auditorium the night of the Financial Town Meeting. They'd rejected the bond four times before. Would they care enough to approve it this time?

"We're gonna win," a man said as he stopped by her chair. He gave her a thumbs-up and moved on.

Kelly frowned, trying to remember his name, then shrugged. She'd met so many people this week that their faces were just a blur.

Elliot folded himself into the seat on Bertie's other side. "The place is packed," he said as he hooked his arm around the cook's shoulders.

But have they come to vote yes, or no? Kelly wondered. She wished suddenly, passionately, that David was here, with his arm around her shoulders, sharing the suspense with her. Bertie didn't know how lucky she was. *Or maybe she does.* Kelly noted the soft smile on her friend's face. *I hope she does.* Somebody ought to be smart enough to recognize a miracle when it was offered. But that thought was too painful to pursue.

Even by West Dartmouth standards, the meeting was long, noisy and passionate. Before they could vote on the bond to build the high school, the town had to vote on the rest of the yearly budget. Speaker after speaker had to have his say, then each item had to be brought to the vote.

Finally, near midnight, the drooping audience sat up straighter and a murmur of excitement swept the room. It was time for the vote on the building bond. *Time for a miracle!* Kelly prayed as Ellen May stood up to give the school committee's plea for a yes vote.

Leland Howard followed, voicing the town council's opinion that the old school was good enough, and that split sessions and reduced school hours had never hurt any serious student.

The head of the teachers' union delivered a passionate rebuttal, then an aging and belligerent gentleman cast a pox on both houses, leaving the audience wondering which way the speaker himself planned to vote.

The last one at the podium was Kelly, her courage hat twisted tight in her hands. This was her final contrition, the last effort she could make for David's cause, but that didn't make it any less painful. "This d-doesn't come down to falling plaster, or overcrowded classrooms, or rising property taxes, or shortened school days for your kids," she stammered. "It...it comes down to this—pure and simple. *Do you care?*"

She scanned the sea of faces beyond the microphone. "These are your kids and the kids of your neighbors. For better or worse, they're family—this whole town is family, even when we squabble. And *you've got to care about your family*. So if you care, and I know you do, *please* vote yes on this bond issue. Thank you." She hurried back to her seat, her cheeks flaming as a thunderous ovation rocked the room.

The motion to vote on the issue was made and seconded. "All those in favor?" the town moderator asked in his dry voice.

"Aye!" Kelly yelled—and was drowned out by the shou
of agreement around her.

"We've got it!" Bertie shrieked in her ear. "I think we'
got it!"

But she clutched Elliot's arm as the moderator said, "A
those opposed?"

The nays were almost as deafening as the ayes. Almos
Kelly told herself. Surely they hadn't been louder?

The moderator looked nervously around the room. "
think the ayes—"

"No!" yelled someone down front and was seconded b
a dozen angry voices. "I move for a standing vote on the i
sue!"

"I second the motion! We want a head count!" someo
else cried.

"All those in favor of passing the bond to build the hig
school, please stand and remain standing until you've be
counted," intoned the moderator.

Kelly stood and two-thirds of the room rose with her
then broke into a roar of triumph. "We've won!" Kel
cried as she hugged Bertie. Pounding her on the back whi
the cook hugged Elliot, she kept on chanting, "We won, w
did it!" All around them, people were laughing, embra
ing, shaking fists at the ceiling in victory, dancing in th
aisles.

And then somehow Kelly's eyes were drawn to the o
face in the whole auditorium that mattered. Standing ne
the far wall, David Whittaker stared back at her, unsm
ing.

"David!" she gasped, though of course he couldn't hea
Deaf to Bertie's questions, she pushed past the cook a
started across the room, her eyes locked on his. *David!*
wave of joy and sheer terror swept through her. All she kn
for certain was that she had to touch him, hear his voic

)h, please! she prayed, and then, *Thank you!* when he tarted forward to meet her.

It took them almost five minutes to reach each other. eople slapped them on the back, gave them high fives and ıumbs-up, yelled every kind of praise and congratula-ons. Kelly simply smiled, nodded and kept on ducking round all the bodies that stood between her and David.

They met in the aisle at the back of the room. David's face 'as wary, almost angry in its lack of expression. His hands ere clenched at his sides. Seeing no welcome, Kelly hugged erself protectively. But after her last rejection, it was up to er to make the first move, wasn't it? With a gulp and a rayer, she flung her arms wide and hugged him.

He stood unmoving, his body rigid against her, then owly, his arms rose to wrap around her and hold her tight. /ith the crowd cheering, all Kelly could hear was, *Thank ɔu, oh, thank you!* pealing in her own brain. All she could el was the pounding of David's heart against her breast, nd the surge of joy that threatened to lift her out of his rms and float her up to the ceiling.

David's lips found her ear. "Hiya, Red," he growled, ugging her again.

"Why did you go?" she cried into a lull in the uproar.

He brushed her ear with his lips. "Sunshine was in a car ccident. Just a broken wrist and a concussion," he added uickly when she pulled back to stare at him in horror.

Just then the moderator announced, "The ayes have ,012 votes," and the ayes burst into another storm of self-ɔngratulation.

"Let's get out of here!" David shouted in her ear.

As they hurried out the exit, the nays were getting to their et with the sullenness of the defeated. Kelly looked back see Leland Howard standing with an ugly scowl on his

face, then she and David pushed through the doors into t
blessed silence of the lobby.

"So Sunshine's all right. Oh, David, I'm so glad!" s
cried as he towed her along by the hand. "And we won! V
really won!"

"I hear you had a lot to do with that," he said, smilin
as he ushered her out into the warm moonlit night.

"It was the least I could do after being such an idiot, l
ting Leland use me like that," she said as they hurried do
the steps. "I should have listened to you."

"That would be a first!" he pointed out dryly. He led h
to his pickup, which was parked on the verge of the ro
with the other vehicles that hadn't fit into the school pa
ing lot.

"And I should have trusted you," she added softly, as s
slid past the door he'd opened for her and into the se
"I'm so sorry about that, David. If I'd used my brains,
my eyes—" *or my heart* "—I would have known you
never do anything dishonest. It's just that—"

"I know." He put a finger to her lips, stopping the wor
"I know." Gently he closed her door.

He stayed silent as he chose a road unfamiliar to Ke
Wondering, but content to go wherever he wanted to ta
her, she studied his frowning profile. He was thinking ha
about something.

She looked up as the truck stopped, to find he had driv
them to the town beach. Beneath a three-quarter moon
line of crinkled silver marked the curve of the shore as
as the eye could see. David came around to her door a
opened it. "I owe you an apology, too," he said as she s
out to stand toe-to-toe with him. "I've been thinking of y
as another Willow."

"Sunshine's mother?" she guessed, kicking off her sho

"Right." Taking her arm, he led her down to the bea
They reached the wavering line where moon-silvered wa

washed up on the sand, then retreated with a soft hiss. Arms locked around each other, they walked that silver-and-black dividing line, Kelly getting her feet wet, David treading the dry sand just above. "Anyway, I watched Willow while I hung around the hospital this week, and I realized how wrong I was," he continued. "You two are a lot alike in the superficial ways. But not in the important ones."

"What's she like?"

"She's your archetypal California free spirit—the flower-child daughter of beatnik parents. A vegetarian like you, only spacier—crystals and astrology and communing with spirits, and Lord knows what all. I thought it was sort of charming when we first dated in college. But once...once we got pregnant, when I realized that she had no intention of marrying me—or marrying anybody..." He let out an angry breath. "That she had no intention of settling down and making a commitment to anything but her whim of the moment..."

"Must have been hard," Kelly sympathized.

"You could say that," he agreed wryly. "She led me on for quite a few years. I kept hoping she'd grow up and see reason. And she, well, she liked having a part-time, no-strings-attached lover. But she wasn't about to tie herself down to one man forever. Finally I realized that and gave it up. Since then, I've been a father on the sidelines. She lets me pay child support, and in return, she lets me see Sunshine, but it's not the same as a family. It's not what I want."

"And how are she and I different?" Kelly asked softly, nudging him higher up the sand as a wave licked his shoes.

"She's a butterfly," he said, "flitting from flower to flower. She's never going to alight anywhere for long. She's even getting tired of being a mother, I think. She talked about moving to Hawaii, or maybe Bali or New Zealand. She wouldn't say yet, but I think—I'm praying—that if I bankroll that adventure, she'll let me have Sunshine for her high-school years."

"Oh, David, I'm so glad for you!" Kelly turned to give him a proper hug. "Then you'll have a family!" What he'd wanted all along, she realized at last. But did he need anything—anyone—more? "You were saying I'm different?" she prompted, looking up at him.

"Yes. You *do* alight," he said, "then start improving madly." There was an undertone of laughter in his voice. His arms tightened around her.

"Like a broody hen," she agreed. "I feather my nest."

He laughed outright. "Something a little more graceful I'd have said. A bluebird, if the coloring wasn't wrong. But yes, that's exactly it. You nest." He traced the curve of her spine with a fingertip. "I've always liked the idea of a nest. Someplace safe and cozy to come home to."

And so do I, she thought, trying to make out the expression in his moon-touched eyes. *We're not so different at all, are we?*

They both started as a wave washed over their ankles. With a laugh, David stepped out of her arms and took off his shoes. They left them to dry above the high watermark and wandered on, hand in hand. "From that message you left with my sitter," Kelly said after a long silence, "I thought you'd gone for good. That you weren't coming back."

"Would you have cared if I hadn't?" David asked, his voice too casual.

"Yes," she confessed softly, then retreated from that confession. "You're my friend."

His voice hardened. "You make friends easily, in case you haven't noticed."

Shy, awkward Kelly Bouchard made friends easily? It was hard to believe, but looking back over the past few months, yes, suddenly life seemed rich with wonderful people. "Bu none like you," she said, her fingers curling tighter around his.

"What kind of friend am I?" David demanded, pulling her to face him.

The kind I could love. There. There it was in all its terrifying glory. She could love him, and if David couldn't love her back, she'd be lost and lonely forever, no matter how many friends she made. The enormity of the words closed her throat and she stared at him helplessly.

He waited, and when she still didn't speak, he let her go. Overhead, a veil of cloud drifted across the moon and the light went out, leaving them stranded in chilly darkness. "No, I was coming back," he said at last, his voice almost harsh. "I've still got some unfinished business here."

It hurt when she swallowed. "Wh—what's that?"

"You..." David said, moving so close that their bodies almost touched. "'Cause like it or not, Kelly Bouchard, ready or not, I'm going to court you."

Her laugh sounded more like a sob, and she shook her head at the sheer wonder of it. *Oh, David!* He was going to give her that second chance?

He caught her shoulders. "I am, Kelly! You can date me *un*seriously if you like, but me, I've never been more serious. I want you in my bed. I want you in my life. It's as pure and simple as that."

"As simple as that?" Joy shimmered in her voice as he rocked her forward and kissed her.

As simple as that! his kiss replied. Twin heartbeats echoed the vow as their bodies twined together and held. Around their ankles, the waves glittered and streamed as the moon danced out from hiding.

Their lips parted in a laughing gasp for air, and Kelly buried her face in his shoulder. She inhaled shakily while he brushed his face back and forth through her hair. "You know," she murmured, "I've been thinking since you've been gone, thinking a lot, and . . . about that courtship?"

"Hmm?" He lifted her face to kiss the tip of her nose then her smile.

"Could we make it a short one?" she asked, laughing and kissed him back.

And so they did.

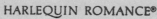

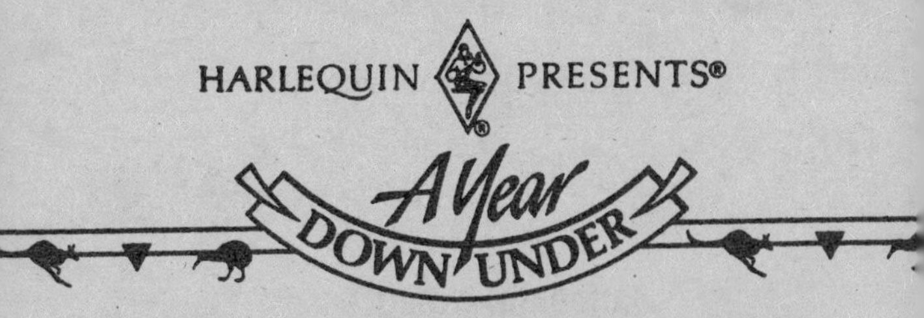

In 1993, Harlequin Presents celebrates the land down under. In March, let us take you to Northland, New Zealand, in THE GOLDEN MASK by Robyn Donald, Harlequin Presents #1537.

Eden has convinced herself that Blade Hammond won't give her a second look. The grueling demands of trying to keep the sheep station running have left her neither the money nor the time to spend on pampering herself. Besides, Blade still considers her a child who needs protecting. Can Eden show him that she's really a woman who needs his love . . . ?

Share the adventure—and the romance—
of A Year Down Under!

Available this month in
A YEAR DOWN UNDER

NO GENTLE SEDUCTION
by Helen Bianchin
Harlequin Presents #1527
Wherever Harlequin books are sold.

YDUF